THE SINS OF SAVAGES: AN URBAN STANDALONE

WRITTEN BY:

MS. STREET CRED

The Sins of Savages: An Urban Standalone

Copyright © 2019 by Ms. Street Cred

All rights reserved.

Published in the United States of America.

The Sins of Savages: An Urban Standalone

Published by Twyla T. Presents, LLC.

Dedicated to:

The lost Youth

Prologue

-Nero-

"If that fuck nigga the one who killed them,I want his head!" Zai voiced through gritted teeth. As he paced back and forth, I for one had heard the conversation between Coach B and his brother, Tone, also; and it sounded very incriminating. My mind was lowkey blown, had we really just overheard our mentor and basketball coach for the last few years, confess to killing our mothers. The shit was beyond me and had me really thinking about a lot of shit now. We tried to rationalize what we really heard and it was no doubt that we were telling the girls. Given that both their parents were murdered, it was our cousinly duty to tell them we finally knew something about our parent's death. All these years without answers, standing in front of news conference cameras, all those sleepless nights we had, and their killer had been looking out for each of us. Had Coach B really murdered the one person that had always been there for me?

I couldn't sleep at all tonight; I tossed and turned as the same recurring dream kept me awake. I just remembered waking up Christmas morning six years ago after burying the charred remains of my mama and aunties and realizing that Christmas would never be the same for me. The shit had been so hard at eight years old and even now it still was hard to cope with. I often wondered if I hadn't lost my mother, would I be pushing dope for one of the biggest drug dealers in the city? I would never know because my mother was never coming back. My Grandma Janice was all I had in this world; my dad had done fifteen years and had been in jail before I was even born. He was just released a few weeks ago. Besides the occasional letters from him, we didn't have any type of bond. Zai always told me I was lucky my dad was still alive because his dad had been murdered the year before our mothers when we were seven; just like Desire and Destiny he had no parents. To me, my dad didn't exist because he hadn't been there. Letters didn't amount to time, the nigga never even let me come see him. My mama had been all I had known besides my grandma and now with her getting older in age, I felt like I'd join my surrogate cousins in being alone completely.

Zai and I stayed in the streets, and I knew my mother wouldn't approve of my lifestyle. She had always instilled in me the importance of school and being more than her and my dad. The way life had gone, it had tossed me smack dab in the middle of the vicious street life. I was going to sell so much dope, I'd be able to afford everything I needed in due time. We had been out in these St. Pete streets since our eleventh birthdays. While we were far too young to be exposed to some of the shit we had been around; when the streets were raising you it was expected. I sat up in my bed staring at the newspaper article that I had taped to my wall. Looking at all five of their faces, I would never forget them. They had all been in our lives since we were born for the most part but the day that they no longer were, still hurt. If Coach B was the one responsible for ending their lives, he was going to pay for their lives with his own. On my mama, he was going to feel my pain.

Chapter One

-Zai-

"Shit! There go twelve!" Dinero yelled as everybody that had been sitting on the wall took off in opposite directions. I kicked my sack of weed and the pistol I was holding, under a city-issued garbage can before taking off down the alley. Them crackas wasn't about to catch a young nigga today. I took off like I had rocket fluid in my J's. As soon as I hit the corner and took off near Emmerson, an undercover cop car was bending the corner. I refused to do another stint in juvie, my Grandma Gladys would kill me if she had to go back in another court room and listen to all the shit I had been into yet again. I slowed my sprint down to a brisk walk as I ducked off into the corner store and peeled a couple dollars off the small knot I had in my pocket. Zaire was what my mama named me but everybody in the neighborhood called me Lil Zeke, after my, dad or these lil thotties called me Zai.

I was always in some shit with my surrogate cousin, Dinero or Nero. We had been thuggin it a long time since our mama's died. All we had was our grandmas and ourselves. Our other surrogate cousins were girls and they were tougher than me and Nero combined. Destiny and Desire stayed fighting lil bitches throughout the neighborhood. If Desire's sticky finger ass saw something she wanted, she was taking it. Destiny dibbled in a lot of illicit activities and didn't care who knew it. Dinero and I were both fourteen and Destiny was older than us all at sixteen and her little sister, Desire, was the youngest out the clique at ten. Yeah, I'm sure a few people would turn their noses up at how me and my cousins conducted ourselves in society, but we were direct products of our environment. All four of us had been the poster children for the most talked about crime in the city back then.

My moms, Dinero's mom, Destiny and Desire's mama and daddy and our auntie Ta'Rhonda, had all been murdered during the holidays six years prior. When we were younger we hadn't gotten all the gruesome details that surrounded their murderers but as we got older, the hood had a way of ruining our innocence for good by repeat shares of the details on social media as well as us all using the internet to our advantage to really see what happened. I just remember that the caskets were all closed. I never got to see what she looked like. I always kept the news article on my wall to remind me of what my mother, Shadequa, looked like. I wouldn't have wished what me and my cousins had gone through, on my worst enemy. We all had been forced to grow up faster than we wanted. Any and every promise that I had made to my mother at the tender age of eight, had since been broken. She had always thought I'd be more than a street hustler like my daddy or a scammer like her but here I was, slanging dope on the block with one of three people that understood my pain.

"Sam, you got any fresh chicken cooking?" I said, eyeing the dry ass chicken in the display case.

"Yeah man, it's coming," the store owner, Sam, responded with a heavy middle eastern accent.

I simply went to the back coolers to grab me a peach Nehi soda and waited for the fresh chicken to come up. While I had been raised off home cooked meals, convenience store food had been feeding me for the last four years. My grandma would cook occasionally but Grandma Gladys wasn't much of a cook anymore. After burying her only child, my grandma had mentally checked out and functioned enough to keep me out of the system. I pulled my Kyocera flip phone that I paid a crackhead ten dollars for, out of my front pocket and checked for any new customers. I had given my burner number out to a few new potential customers at the RibFest downtown last week. People would be surprised how much of our country were really addicted to some kind of drug. Hella mu'fuckas were snorting bathsalt, sticking Lortabs down their throats, and people were even bringing back a classic favorite by reviving the shooting up of heroin.

All I did was smoke a lil weed but I didn't like how it made me feel and only did it occasionally. Nero stayed high but I knew he was trying to mask the pain he felt. I combatted my pain with that drank. I stayed sipping lean and loved how it slowed me down when I thought I was just running. I also enjoyed a nice stiff cup of whiskey, no chaser. Jack Daniels was my poison. I could bathe in a tub of Jack; my first time drinking it had been the best night of my life and I often recreated that exact vibe anytime I had the pleasure of getting a personal bottle.

"Yo Zai wassup, man?" a nigga from the neighborhood said as he paid for his Newports and his lotto tickets

"Wassup Pete," I said, seeing the fresh chicken being brought out by Sam's wife, Aanisah. My mouth instantly started watering.

I got the hood special which was five wings and fries for five dollars and the wings were huge! I paid for my drink and food and thanked Sam before exiting the store. I fumbled with holding all my items and searching for my iPhone XR that was deep down in my pocket. I wanted to make sure the block had cooled down or head on home to let the block cool off. Before I could dial his number, Nero's name and face popped up on my screen. I slid the button over to answer.

"Yo cousin, we all at Blocca's come through," Nero said as he debated sports stats with someone in the background.

"I'm on my way fam," I said as I re-entered the store to grab my cousin some food too. This nigga wasn't about to sit up and eat my food today, he was getting his own tray.

Chapter Two

-Desire-

"Hey! Stop her!" the out-of-shape mall security guard yelled distances away as I bolted out the mall's automatic doors. The stolo had was parked to the right of the entrance. While my young ass had no business driving, I was a professional driver. I wasn't a typical ten-year-old. I wasn't into sleepovers, dolls, or dance practice. I was into taking any and everything I could get my little hands on. To sum it up, society would call me a kleptomaniac, I would argue that I simply was taking what I deserved. I hopped in the car and threw the seat back, observing the fat security guard looking around the parking lot. After a few more minutes, he turned and went back inside.

"Whew that was close," I said to myself as I re-adjusted the seat and cranked the car up. At ten, I was much taller than the average girl my age. I stood at 5'3 and had successfully learned how to drive at eight. After a few lessons from my sister, Destiny, I was driving illegally but with the precision of a racecar driver. I drove out the parking lot and was headed south to scoop my sister up from her class at the technical college. I still went to school, but I chose when I wanted to learn. School wasn't for me. I wasn't dumb or anything, I just felt like living life taught me more than school ever could. Fifth grade could come and go, I was ready for middle school.

Destiny and her stable of guys she entertained was an interesting sight to see. We had been groomed by the likes of City Girls and Cardi B when it came to dealing with the opposite sex. While I wasn't into boys just yet, my sister had already filled me in on what was what when it came to these niggas. The only two niggas I trusted were Nero and Zai; they had been like my cousins my whole life. They looked out for me and Destiny and we did the same for them.

They had suffered in the same tragedy as us except they had only lost their mothers. Our mama and daddy were both murdered in the incident labeled by the streets as the Christmas in the Trap Murders. Nobody knew shit when it came to knowing anything about it. And if they did know, they weren't talking. Six years ago, at four years old, I became a motherless child in a world so cold. Our mom's mom didn't fuck with us and our dad's mom had been the one to take us in when everything happened, but my Grandma Bev was still out trying to be twenty-five at fifty-five. She was rarely home, always in somebody bar, and because she was rarely home, me and my sister ran amuck around her house and the neighborhood.

With our home life carefree, Destiny and I had been propelled head-first into doing whatever we wanted, whenever we wanted. Sometimes our grandma would be gone for weeks at a time with one of her suitors she had picked up at a bar, forgetting she had responsibilities at home. We wouldn't see or talk to her. She would stock the house up for us and leave a few dollars but otherwise, our grandma was living her best life. While others would say she was neglecting us, me and my sister appreciated the freedom. Plus, as long as we had each other and the boys, we were good.

I pulled up to Pinellas Technical school or, PTEC to those that were from here, I spotted my beautiful older sister standing on the curb, yapping away on her phone. I hopped over in the passenger seat as she walked around the car and got in, continuing her call even after waving at me silently and putting on her seat belt. I sat enthralled on Facebook, watching the latest stories and antics my friends were doing. A few people had gone live and was just shooting the shit on Facebook. I never posted; it was a rare thing for me to interact besides through messenger. I just lurk on here, looking for other people's dramas. They posted it and obviously wanted me to see, so I was always going to look at the drama going on.

I was listening but not listening to Destiny's conversation. Based off how she was talking, I knew it was one of her boo's; more specifically it was her main thing, Mario from the way she said bae. Rio was the only dude that I heard Destiny call bae. Out of all the dudes she messed with, Rio had always looked out when she needed him but he was community dick. My sister had to fight all the time because some bitch was claiming Rio or just disrespecting her when everyone knew Mario wasn't about anything. And while she knew he was a hoe, she still dealt with him. Rio would come around for a couple weeks, then disappear. It would be a matter of time before he wasn't even a topic again.

My sister didn't end her call until we were pulling out front of our grandma's house, and as usual our grandma wasn't home. Making our way inside, Destiny went straight to the kitchen while I went to my room to admire my newest stolen trinket from Kay Jewelers. When I pulled out the one carat diamond tennis bracelet from my pocket, it sparkled in my hand. I don't know what compelled me to snatch it out the old white lady's hand when she pulled it out to show me, but I had to have it. It would pair nicely with the white and gray Fashion Nova set I had Destiny order for me. I admired the beautiful bracelet a second longer before adding it to my growing jewelry collection.

"Hey, wanna run down on Nero and Zai?"

Destiny said from my doorway

"Yeah, I need to smoke," I said

"That's all your young ass wanna do besides taking shit that don't belong to you," my sister said with a slight attitude

"Well let's not forget where I smoked my first blunt at and with who," I said, cutting my eyes at her. Destiny always found the worst times to try and be a big sister, forgetting that she had been the one to introduce all these bad habits to me.

I followed my sister back out the house, in route to the block. Before we arrived, we left the stolo on the side of the street after wiping down the steering wheel, gear shift, and door handle and walking the remainder of the way.

Chapter Three

-Destiny-

Being my little sister's keeper is hard but for the last six years, we have been each other's rock. It was easier telling Desire where she was wrong after she had already committed her crimes in hopes that the next, time she thought about doing something she'd at least think about it. I stood at her room door long enough to see her stash her latest item. Our grandmother, Bev, did under the bare minimum when it came to us. I worked a regular ol' job at McDonald's but I really made my money fucking for cash. At sixteen, I was out there trying to survive while also picking up our caregiver's slack. I looked over to my baby sister as she had her nose all in her phone as we walked. She managed to walk without even looking. She looked like our mom, Anastasia, while I favored our dad, Devaughn. We had heard and read about the gruesome details surrounding their murders but for years, the streets hadn't spoken on who did it. Nero and Zai stayed in the streets, in hopes that one day somebody would fuck up and say something. The day that happened, we'd be masking up to avenge our parents' deaths. Desire had been right though; I would condone certain behavior from not only her but the boys too, and when my conscious kicked in I'd be mad at myself for allowing them to do something I really wasn't down with from the start.

As we neared the block, we could hear Kevin Gates' hit song *"Shoulda"* blasting from a car parked out front of the trap where Nero and Zai posted up. If they weren't here, they were at the wall around the corner by the park. They posted up either places when the time and situation permitted, I could spot Zai from a mile away, the kid was fresh and looked exactly like his dad, Zeke. Zai could relate to us completely given he too had no one but his grandma. Ms. Gladys was just like our grandma; doing just enough to keep him out the foster care system. Yet he was out here in this world, providing for not only himself but for her. Just like me, Zai paid bills in his grandma's house. Yes, at fourteen, Zai was doing more than a grown ass man. Ms. Gladys would protest often but that didn't stop her from taking the money. My grandma on the other hand, had her head so far up these old men's asses that she didn't realize I took care of a lot of shit she was supposed to be doing. The shit was hard sometimes but I knew that I refused to go into foster care and my sister wasn't either.

Desire ran ahead and jumped on Zai's back, knowing the boy was gone complain if any of his fit had gotten dirty. While we all had moments where we were older than we appeared, a ten-year-old was still going to be a kid. Yet if you called Desire a kid or told her she was being childish you would meet a quite different person. I blame the lack of parental guidance for that. Once Zai had finally inspected that there wasn't any dirt on his outfit, he walked over and gave me a half hug. I loved this boy like he was my little brother; he and Nero meant a lot to me just like my sister. We had all bonded over our parents' untimely demises, me being the oldest was tough. Every Christmas, they would run the information reel about someone coming forward with information and for the last six years, no one had ever come forward. It was a cold case now and personally, I felt like the detectives had all but given up. Back then I was the age Desire is now, she had been four at the time of the incident. I don't know how much she remembers, and I've never asked. I knew I had nightmares about it, but I didn't want to trigger her to start if she hadn't been before. At ten, I had been the apple of my daddy's eye and regardless of the scammer type shit my mama was on, her and I had reached pivotal moments in our relationship.

For as long as I could remember, my mama had been a booster. My earliest memory of her had been inside my stroller and being snatched up out of it, so she could stuff clothes underneath me and my blanket. I don't know if a one-and-a-half-year-old could feel embarrassed, but I felt like that. There were countless other incidents that occurred that I remembered. The only reason I really knew what my mama, Auntie Shad, Auntie Ta' Rhonda and Auntie Celeste were really doing was because my grandma on my mama side would be sitting up getting loaded, playing spades with her nosey ass friends while talking shit about my mama. I would wait till I got home and tell my mama what they would say. She would always tell me not to pay Grandma Rita no mind but in the back of my little mind, she was speaking truth about my mama and I was too young to realize it. While I knew our parents loved us, at times we were used as pawns. At ten, I had the latest iPhone. When I was at school, I would know when they'd be around each other. Plus, coming home and smelling the lingering smell of my dad's cologne let me know he had been at our house for some time, especially since their locations stayed on. I couldn't understand why they could get together alone and be just fine but anytime me and Desire were around, they couldn't stand one another. Nero appearing out the trap broke me from my thoughts as he walked straight over to us and attempted to pass me the blunt he had lit. Desire intercepted it right before I could grab it.

"Youngest go first," her childish ass said, backing up and taking quick pulls of the blunt.

I wasn't even about to chase her ass because I knew how to get her lil ass back. After a few more minutes, she walked over with her arm extended with the blunt in my direction. Snatching it from her small hands, I rolled my eyes hard as fuck at her. Sometimes this little girl got on my mu'fuckin nerves.

"Damn ya'll wild man!" Nero said, laughing while shaking his head.

"Man, she started the shit," I said while sucking my teeth before placing the blunt in my mouth and inhaling the smoke.

Desire cut her eyes at me before walking over to the porch, where she got back enthralled into her phone. If her lil ratchet ass friends weren't boosting her up to fight they were up to no good in other places, like taking shit that didn't belong to them. The boys and I were already a bad enough influence on her but them no good ass friends of hers were the worst. While we knew how to control her, they had no clue on how to handle the little demon child that she had become. Desire was the cutest at four but even then, she would cut her eyes at our mama or roll her little eyes. There were times our mama had to remember she was four because the look in her eyes let me know she wanted to snatch her little ass up. Yet, my mama knew Desire had got that shit from her ass and her correcting her rude four-year-old would be like correcting her twenty-eight-year-old self. I honestly think if our mama was still here, she would still be teaching Desire and I unhealthy traits and habits.

By the time the blunt had gone around four times, with Zai declining each time we tried to pass it to him, the three of us were zooted. Desire had since begun to complain that she was hungry and lowkey so was I.

"Ya'll order some pizza and wings and I'll pay for it," Nero said, walking off towards the road to catch a sell.

He didn't have to tell Desire twice, she had Domino's on speed dial.

"Have it delivered to ya'll grandma's house, these greedy ass niggas gone want some," Zai added

"Hell yeah, have that shit brought to Grandma Bev's, we'll just have dinner the four of us," Nero said, walking back up as he looked around to check his surroundings.

Desire put in the order as we agreed to meet them at our grandmother's.

As we headed back home, Desire had to have a snack to hold her over, so we detoured to the store to pick up a few drinks and snacks to go with the food. We knew Nero would come with some bud and that always helped me settle some food. Twenty-five minutes later, the boys arrived and no sooner than they had, the delivery driver was knocking too. Nero paid as promised, and we proceeded to dig in. I loved when a nigga paid, regardless if they were family or not it was what they were supposed to do. At least that's what my daddy had told me. And I believed him till this day.

Chapter Four

-Nero-

This sausage, ham, and bacon pizza was touching a nigga's soul. Even though Zai had brought me a chicken wing tray earlier, a nigga had smoked several blunts since eating that, so the girls being hungry was right on time.

"Yo Des, pour me some of that RC Cola man," I said with a mouth full of food

"Eww Nero, chew with your mouth closed!" Desire yelled at me with her face all screwed up.

"Who was this lil jit yelling at?" I thought to myself. She had a nigga fucked up. I had paid for this mu'fuckin pizza and if I wanted to talk with my mouth full, I was going to do just that.

"Man shut yo ass up, I paid for this mu'fucka," I said, exposing the chewed-up pizza in my mouth

She rolled her eyes at me again before completely looking away with her slice in her hand.

Destiny walked over and handed me a warm cup of soda.

"Sorry no ice, cuz," she said before I could ask.

"Damn I know I'm a hood nigga but warm soda," I said, gulping down the strong acid-filled soda.

"Yo Nero, you coming to practice today?" Zai inquired.

A nigga had real deal been slacking when it came to this basketball shit. I hadn't been to practice all week because a nigga was out catching money. Coach B had to understand.

"Shit cuz, Ima try but you know Dash got that pack coming in today. I'm trying to be the first nigga with my slice of that pie," I told my surrogate cousin.

He simply nodded his head at me as we finished up our food. I knew Zai was trying to get out with this basketball shit. My boy was nice with the rock, but he also could sell some crack too. I felt my phone vibrating in my pocket as I wiped my hands with a napkin before retrieving it. I'd be damned if I got pizza grease on these nearly four-hundred-dollar Evisu jeans. Looking at the screen, I recognized the prison's number. I picked up the call, listening to the automated prompt.

"You have a collect call from "Dee" a prisoner in the Suwannee Correctional Institute. To accept this call press zero, otherwise press one to block all calls from this facility."

I pressed zero and awaited to hear the voice of my dad. He'd been calling me faithfully the last six years. He had called when my mom was still living but sometimes the calls would go unanswered because my mom was still pissed he had left her to raise me alone. Our conversations were always upbeat, and my dad always made a point to encourage me to be better than him.

Dino: "Yoooo son wassup? How's the world treating you?"

Me: "Wassup pops, everything is everything outchea. How they treatin' you in there?"

Dino: "Shit son, they treat a nigga like an inmate."

Me: "You know granny happy you'll be home soon."

Dino: "Yeah I been missing moms, she ain't never brought you to come see me."

Me: "You know how granny is, she don't really drive like that."

Pops and I talked for a few more minutes before the automatic operator told us we had one minute left. Pops promised to call me back in a few days with an update on his release date. I slid my phone on the table and no sooner than I had, it begin to buzz again. Checking the incoming call, I could see it was my latest bae calling. I was still trying to eat my money's worth of this damn pizza, so I shot her one quick text letting her know I'd call her back later.

"When your daddy gettin' out?" Desire asked as she stood to discard her trash.

"Shit that's what I'm still waiting to see, I may have to get one of the big homies to rent me a car so I can go get him."

"Cuz, you know your pops gone be talking shit if yo young ass pull up in a whip," Zai interjected.

He was right though; my pops would have too many questions for a nigga and I wasn't ready to go down that road with him just yet.

"Thank you for dinner, Dinero," Destiny said, collecting Zai and I's plates.

When I thought about my Auntie Stasi, her daughters reminded me of her in many ways but they were also so different from her too. Destiny was the mild-mannered one while Desire was the wild child. Auntie Stasi had been the ratchet one out of the group and I remember my mama always talking with my other aunts about how Auntie Stasi lived and behaved. Luckily for her girls, they both were relatively clean people, but Desire was ratchet as hell when she wanted to be. I remember going to their house when I was little, and all my auntie did was yell at them. I would be so happy when my mom would come pick me up. I often wondered how we all would be right now had they not been murdered. My Auntie Ta'Rhonda, had also been my God mom and an aspiring rapper. I remember her taking me to the studio countless times to watch her record. I missed them all terribly. Destiny continued to clean up as my ringing iPhone brought me back to reality. Recognizing the number, I motioned for Zai. It was time to bounce. We said bye to the girls and headed back to the block. It was going to be a long night.

Chapter Five

-Dino-

Dinner tonight was halfway decent. I mean, it still lacked character or flavor, but it had been better than the shit I had grown accustomed to for the last fifteen years. They had just done count and it was about an hour until lights out. I had barely made it to call my son, Dinero, before the officers were telling us to line up for count. I would say that I was over being treated like a slave, but I had put myself in this predicament. I had never seen my son in the flesh; just through pictures, but I knew his voice. I always was mad at myself for leaving Celeste pregnant with nothing but a few thousand dollars, which she ended up using for my lawyer when I first got locked up. While I had been guilty of the charges of distribution, I had been around the wrong mu'fuckas. Till this day I kicked myself in the ass for being too trusting. It had cost me not only my freedom but also aided in a lot of my depressive state while incarcerated. Talking with my only son and child was the only thing that got me through this time. To say I had been devastated when I got word Celeste had been murdered was an understatement. I honestly felt like I had died. The prison had me sit down with a therapist and everything, but they still denied my request to attend her funeral. After she died, I felt bad that my son had been left as my mom's responsibility. I should have been out to protect them both but at the time, I still had a few more years to go before I'd be free. I just felt like Celeste would have never been caught up in nothing had I been out to be a man.

Yeah, I had heard the story, and the details made me sick. I knew her friends well and had tried on numerous occasions to deter her from them. Yet, her bond with her best friends was stronger and she managed to always get herself in the craziest shit with their asses. I thought once they asses started having kids, they would calm down, but Stasi and Shad just fueled her ratchetness. I had much respect for Ta'Rhonda because she was usually the level-headed one out of the four but she too was with whatever her girls were on. Sadly, they all had lost their lives behind dumb shit. Even though I was locked up all the way in Live Oaks, mu'fuckas in here still talked and there were speculations of who could have done it but why was my biggest question. What had Celeste ass done to be murdered. I knew they boosted but that was minor compared to how violently they were killed. Whoever did it must not have known that my shorty was a mom, cause I just couldn't see anyone doing her like that. I was about two weeks shy of being a free man and I had vowed six years ago that I was going to find whoever did that fuck shit to her and end their life. It could be a female or a male but whomever had pulled the trigger, was going to pay with their life. I laid on my bunk with my hands behind my head as I looked up at the photos I had tucked under the frame of the top bunk. I had lost my bunky, Los, a week prior because he was transferred to another facility. He had been my bunky for the last three years and had helped me mentally get through a lot of shit these last few years.

Los, like most men incarcerated was here on drug charges and had a whole family at home that he had to watch grow while he was behind bars. He was on year four of his twenty-year sentence and had the mental tenacity that I wished I had when I first came in. It had taken me years to gain that type of mental strength and often times I found myself faltering a little. Los taught me even at the age of thirty-four, that men weren't always meant to be strong. It was ok to be in touch with your feelings. I hated that my son was learning life's hard lessons without me. While my mother had been primary caregiver for me when I was growing up, I knew she was getting up in age and not physically built to chase behind a teenager. I had been hearing things in the grapevine about a few young niggas running the streets in Da Burg. A few of the old heads in here told me they had heard my son was involved with them. That hurt me to my heart, and I prayed that he wasn't. I knew he would have the hustler's gene by default. Celeste and I had embedded it in him without even trying.

I was counting the days that I was set to be released just so I could confirm or deny what I was hearing. I prayed to God that Dinero was being cautious if he was in the streets. I was going to make it my mission to get him out of the street life. I had spent enough of my life in confinement to know I never wanted my son to be here. As I thought about my impending release, I heard the on-duty guard announce it was lights out. I got comfortable on my bunk as I got ready to sleep for a few hours. I hoped these two weeks flew by.

Chapter Six

-Bandy-

"Alright Zaire, good hustle today!" I said, watching him run off the court and straight to his Nike gym bag.

"Thanks Coach B, I'm trying to get better with my driving to the basket," he said, putting his attention on his phone.

I had let the other players go early, so I could work with one of my star players. Zaire had the ambition to be one of the greatest basketball star's the state had ever seen. I knew with a little more practice, he could take his talents to college. I had started a rec center designed to keep kids off the streets. I had invested a lot of my drug money into building the H. Daniels Rec Center. I had since slowed my activity in the streets for the last few years. I had entrusted the game to my younger brother, Tone, and his best friend, Dash. I was still their plug and made sure the streets were flooded with the best of the best, but I was trying to focus on making my money more legit. I had always wanted to give back to my community and what better way to do so than to build a safe haven for the kids in the city. I had been living in Tampa for the past few years but decided to relocate to the city that had made me, when this property became available. I also needed to be close to the four souls that I had robbed of happiness. Being able to watch each of them as they grew only inspired me more to open this center. They had been left to fend for themselves because of me. I had been the person to end the lives of their parents. I thought back to the night I watched the breaking news banner come up on the late-night news.

I was finally back in Brandon after collecting all their shares but one. I was willing to take that loss because I had gotten my satisfaction from taking each and every one of their lives. A breaking news story flashed across Bay News Nine. I unmuted the TV and turned it up a bit, listening as the newscaster spoke.

"Police officials in St. Petersburg are working to discover the identities of five bodies recovered from an abandoned house that was set on fire late last night or early this morning. Police aren't yet sure on the details, but we plan to keep you updated as this is a developing story."

I smiled at the TV and took a slow drag off my Backwood. I was one bad man, but nobody or no one would ever get one up on me. This Christmas was about principles, and no one would ever try me like they had again.

Zaire broke my thoughts for a moment as he walked over and dapped me and my assistant coach up. He was probably headed to the block to catch up with his right hand, Dinero. Nero had been missing more and more practices and he too, could ball. He was so enthralled in what my brother and Dash had him pushing that he had all but forgotten about being a kid. I was the reason he was more into the streets than into being a normal fourteen-year-old. I remembered when I had jumped off the porch and the money kept me from doing what my mom wanted. I had been hustling for nearly fifteen years and had seen and done a lot and while my mother was still alive and well, these jits had nobody to stay on their asses. Every time I looked at Zaire, I saw his mom, Shad. While she had been beautiful to look at, she had been dumb to think that her and her friends could steal from me and live to talk about it. After the first year, I had the uncontrollable need to make sure all they shorties were straight. I had my brother hype them up about joining my basketball team when they first started hanging around the block and at first, Zaire had declined but Dinero was at practice faithfully. Now their roles had been reversed and not even Zaire could get Dinero to show up for practice. The daughters of Devaughn and Anastasia had been super active in other programs at the rec center. After a while Destiny, who at the time was twelve, decided that she didn't want to be a cheerleader. Naturally her little sister, who had been six, wanted to follow in her sister's footsteps.

I knew that Destiny was now entertaining a few guys that didn't necessarily mean her any good but with my watchful eye on her, I wouldn't allow them niggas to do anything that brought harm to her or her sister. They all had grandmothers but those old ass bitties did just enough to keep getting them government checks. I had been keeping tabs on everyone involved in their lives, which wasn't many. I knew Desire was one stunt away from being in JDC and that didn't surprise me, given who her mother was. The boys were slowly rising in street ranks and my brother made a point to remind me every chance he got. I looked at the clock on the wall of my closet. I came back from my thoughts as I finished my business at the rec center before locking up and heading home. My live-in girlfriend, Mia, was probably at home waiting on me to get in so I could fuck her brains out. She had come into my life at the right time, in my opinion. The murderers, while I would die believing they were justified, had put me in such a dark space. I had been having recurring dreams since that week of terror. I was always strong; the streets had made me numb to a lot of shit but leaving four kids as orphans had taken a toll on me. Mia had been pumping gas at the Thorton's on Thirty Fourth street and I had just pulled in to meet with one of the rap artist that I worked with. I had been so into watching her thick ass pump her gas that I hadn't even seen my dawg pull up beside me.

Till this day, Charli would clown me for how I had been so consumed by the thick peanut butter-complexioned Queen sporting the Thrasher bodysuit and matching Vans. I hadn't noticed his ass parked beside me for the duration it took her to pump her gas and twist the gas cap back on, before hopping out my own whip and getting her number. I had only noticed him when I turned to return to my own vehicle, in which he was shaking his head and laughing at me. Mia had really opened my heart and mind to a lot, and I was so lucky and blessed to have her. I navigated to my condo in Pasadena, watching the hood change into manicured lawns. I was thinking about the day I could fully wash my hands of this street shit for good. I was older now and Mia was looking less like a girlfriend to me and more like a wife. She catered to a nigga like how Beyoncé and them other girls sang about in their one song. It was starting to all make sense for me and I just saw beyond supplying my little brother. Besides, Tone had proven himself ever since he fucked up all those years ago. Had him and Dash been more seasoned, they would have never been caught slipping and because they had slipped, that resulted in the gruesome murders to begin with.

As I pulled into my designated spot at the Pasadena Cove Condominiums, it was quiet per usual. That was one thing about living amongst white folks; there weren't noisy neighbors or ghetto ass shit going on all night. My humble beginnings had afforded me the luxury to live amongst some of our countries one percenters and I sure as hell wasn't going back to anything less. As I entered my unit, my nostrils practically led me to the kitchen where I found the crock pot on low with my favorite meal stewing away. My mouth watered at the sight of the oxtails, carrots, and potatoes simmering away. I noticed the white rice on the stove and I naturally wanted to fix my plate, but I knew it wasn't done. Mia would kill me if I disturbed her cooking process. Speaking of my beautiful girlfriend, she had yet to show her face as I finally set my keys and phone on the counter and headed further into our two-bedroom condo. As I got closer to our room, I could hear retching coming from the bathroom before pushing the ajar bathroom door further open. I found Mia on her knees, emptying the contents of her stomach into the toilet. I turned into the caring boyfriend as I rubbed her back and tried coaching her through her sudden sickness as she cried and vomited. I hadn't noticed the First Response pregnancy test until I reached over to the towel rack to retrieve a washcloth to wet.

Mia was looking up from the toilet with regret as she saw my caring nature instantly turn cold. I forgot all about making sure she was ok as I left her in the bathroom to get herself together. I went out into the living room and poured myself a glass of 1738 as I plopped down on the couch. I processed what had just been revealed to me void of any words. Yeah, I loved her, but I had been quite clear in explaining that I didn't want kids early on in our relationship. I had been watching four children without parents for the last few years and that was all the parenting I was trying to do. I owe them all that much, but the thought of having my own kids was never an option. If my karma was to come, I knew that one day my fate would be sealed. I would be damned if I left a seed in this world to figure it out without me. I had deserted the idea of being a parent the moment I secretly started looking out for Nero, Zai, Desire, and Destiny. I vowed to be there for all of them as long as I have breath in my body. It wasn't because I wanted to, but I felt I had to. Mia didn't know what I had done but she knew I didn't want any kids. I downed the drink, still stuck on the couch. As I stood to fix another, Mia finally emerged with a flushed face and her Brazilian Remy disheveled on top of her head.

"Baby, I know how you feel about kids, but I wanna keep it," she said as she leaned against the doorframe, leading to our room.

My jaws tightened just hearing her express that she actually wanted to keep it. I pinched the bridge of my nose, trying not to hurt her feelings. She slowly made her way over to sit in the Gianna accent chair that dwelled off to the side of the room. I watched her intensely as she pulled her legs under her with tears forming in her eyes. She knew what I was about to say, yet she had fixed her gaze on me as if she was expecting me to say something different. I took another swig of my drink before I finally spoke.

"Baby you know I love you, but we've been over this too many times for me to count. You must like seeing me mad?" I asked, staring right at her from my position on the couch. She was playing with the drawstrings on her shorts and fighting back tears.

"Brodrick, why is it that you can give me everything I don't want but the one thing I want, you want me to not have? Am I not good enough to be the mother to your kids? We've been together nearly five years now!" she said with hurt and anger behind her words

I felt bad for denying her the one thing she wanted which was to be a mother and while she possessed all the things I would want as a wife and mother; I just could not allow her to do this.

"Mia you can't have this baby, I'm sorry. You know how I feel about this issue and I'm not budging on this. We going to get an abortion, that's final."

I watched as the tears she had been fighting back begin to fall freely down her flushed face.

"Fuck You Bandy! I'm not getting another abortion, you don't fuckin' love me! If you did, you wouldn't dare keep asking me to put my body through fuckin' abortions!" she screamed before retreating into our bedroom.

I sat in the same spot for a few more minutes, thinking about what she had just said and while I felt bad for giving her an ultimatum I knew it was for the best. This would be her third abortion since we had been together. As I prepared to have another drink, Mia came walking out of our room with her Eddie Bauer overnight bag in tow. She cut her eyes at me as she headed towards the door. She said nothing as she stormed out, leaving me with a half a bottle of Remy and my own thoughts.

Chapter Seven

-Desire-

"Stop with the loose talk

That's how bitches get dog walked

They found out who they fucking with and try to call the beef off

I finish bitches off, have yo body outlined in chalk

Opps trying to small talk, you bitches is cotton soft

The Molly make niggas stall

On the block, 6 o'clock

You know we all got chops"

As Molly Brazy's voice blared in my ears through the latest version of air pods I swiped from a white boy in my class. I walked to my fourth period, full from lunch. My girl, Onisha, was walking beside me with her nose practically in her phone most likely trolling on Facebook. I was watching my surroundings as I plotted on my next item. I had peeped Patrice's pussy ass putting her apple watch in her backpack earlier from P.E. and she still hadn't returned it to her wrist, so I called dibs on it amongst our group of friends. Onisha and Javeeka already had Apple watches and Bryson's gay ass had yelled he wanted it a second too late, so he would have to wait his turn for another opportunity to get him one. I had my sights on Patrice's pink fatigued Jansport backpack and I was going to have that watch by the time fourth period was over. Nisha and Veeka were both in their own little worlds but I was focused on the moment I could snatch that watch out the front pocket of Patrice's backpack. Bryson was always with helping one of us obtain some shit we wanted, so he was going to distract her before we made it to the library for our media class. We got closer to our designated building. Patrice, who had been laughing with her group of lame friends, parted ways from them finally and stopped at the water fountain to fill her water bottle. She dropped her backpack to the ground after retrieving her water bottle, and Bryson took that opportunity to walk over to her and start a bullshit ass conversation. Veeka and Nisha just kept walking as I took the time to purposely drop my mechanical pencil down near the bag. With one foul swoop, I unzipped the bag and right on top rested the watch. Bryson cut his eyes at me once as he was asking Patrice a question about an assignment they had due in another class. I smirked at him before cuffing the watch and zipping the front pocket back.

I kept it moving, bending the corner just as Bryson closed his binder and leaving Patrice to finish her task. He caught up with me as we neared the library.

"Now bitch I want the same energy when it's my turn to snag me one," he said as he playfully rolled his eyes. I had to admit, I owed Bryson a lot. He was always clutch when any of us needed him.

"Best friend, you know I got you. I'll steal it myself if I have to," I said honestly.

We talked until we made it into the already rowdy classroom that was located in the library. Our regular teacher Ms. Hansley was out sick, so we had a substitute. We all knew we weren't going to be doing any type of work today and the substitute who looked like he'd rather be anywhere but there, was nose-deep in his iPhone. I looked down at my own phone as I took notice of the time. My grandma would be picking me up soon for a dentist appointment that I was dreading. As I got comfortable in my seat to wait out the next thirty minutes in anticipation for my grandma, Patrice walked in just as the bell rung. We both shot each other dirty looks but mine came attached with a smirk. I couldn't wait to sport my new Apple watch. As everyone got into their own zone, our substitute kicked back in the swivel chair he was in and put his feet on the desk as he got deeper into his. Bryson tapped me every few seconds to show me something he saw on his Instagram feed. Between looking from my phone and back at his, I finally heard the secretary from the front office call over the intercom for me to go. I snatched my backpack up and headed out the door. As I touched the handle, I caught a glimpse of Patrice frantically searching through her front pocket of her backpack. I smirked one last time before exiting the classroom and heading to the office to meet my grandma.

"Desire, you gotta stop giving them people a hard time every time we go to these damn appointments. Yo ass a badass in them damn streets but can't handle a damn dentist inspecting your mouth."

My Grandma Bev ranted to herself because I wasn't listening. I didn't care about her opinion when it came to me damn nearly punching the dentist every time we went to an appointment. I didn't like how they handled my damn teeth and I never would. I really hated when they would try and floss my damn teeth; that was my least favorite part. I slid my Air pods in my ears the rest of the ride home, hoping her phone would ring with a call from one of her many boyfriends. Fifteen minutes later, my grandma swung her 2019 Cadillac in our driveway as she waited impatiently for me to get out. I slammed the car door as I made my way up to the porch. As I snatched one of the wireless ear bulbs out of my ear, I could hear my grandma talking shit about me slamming her door as she pulled back out of the driveway. I didn't care; she was really getting on my nerves. I know if my mama was still there, I would be much happier. I could swing my attitude around when I was little, and my mama wouldn't bat an eye. I used the spare key my grandma had given each of us. I walked in to my sister's sex moans coming from her room. I purposely slammed the door to stop whatever was happening behind her closed door. Within minutes, she was out of her room with a pink cheetah print throw wrapped around her lower half and her hair a mess on her head. She looked around, expecting to see our grandma but when she saw me she gave me a dirty look before retreating back to her room.

I was going to intentionally post up in the living room to catch whoever was making Destiny scream and moan all through the house. While I wasn't interested in letting any boy touch me, I did have a crush on a boy in the neighborhood that played on the rec center basketball team with Nero and Zai. Wakeem was the color of a chicken patty and I had been crushing him since last summer when he first joined the team. From what my friends said, he was really good at the sport and was always braggin' that he was going to the NBA. I had stopped going to that rec center. I was very tempted in going back but they had no programs I liked and after cheer and dance didn't work out, I quit when Destiny stopped going. Nero had been the most consistent but now he didn't even go. I channel surfed a bit until I heard Destiny come out looking crazy once again, but this time with a pair of shorts on and her hair a little more tamed. She smacked her lips and rolled her eyes at me as a new face emerged from the darkness of her room. I smirked at her as she hurriedly rushed her new suitor out of the front door. Seconds later, she stood in front of me.

"Yo lil ass ain't slick. You need to get chu some bidness!" she said with an attitude.

"Girl bye! I don't know what you talkin bout, I just wanted to watch TV," I replied, trying my hardest not to crack a smile.

Even at ten, I was slicker than oil and my sister was probably the only one who could call my bluff, but today I refused to fold. Her ass had gotten caught and was probably embarrassed. She stormed off back to her room, where I heard her slam her door. I finally released the smile I had been holding and turned off the TV before heading to my own room.

The Next Day

"Desire, your lil boo balled out last night," Javeeka said playfully as we sat in P.E. waiting for the bell for lunch.

"Girl he ain't my boo," I said, finally exposing my wrist with the pink Apple Watch on it. I had successfully synced it last night before bed and had picked my pink 95' Air Max to match with it. This was my first time even showing my friends.

"Oooh you bold, bold," Onisha said as she texted away on her phone.

"I can't wait till ya'll help me get one," Bryson chimed in.

"I told you friend, I will," I said as I slid my jacket sleeve back down re-hiding my stolen item.

"Soooo Desire you really gonna act like you ain't checking for Wakeem?" Javeeka asked again, stirring the pot.

"I said no, why?" I asked, checking my phone for the time. The bell should have been going off any minute for lunch, I was starving.

"Well then if you don't want his fine ass, I'ma just shoot my shot then," she said with a smirk.

I cut my eyes at her and said, "Bitch if you ever violate our friendship like that, I'll beat the fuck outta yo ass!"

with a straight face an attitude. Bryson and Onisha both had the ol shit faces displayed before Javeeka could say anything

"Damn Desire, I was just joking," she said with a little sadness in her voice. As she prepared to gather her things, the bell sounded off and we all grabbed our backpacks to head to lunch. I walked ahead to be first in line because it was chicken parm day and I liked mine fresh as possible. Bryson and Onisha were a few people behind me, and Javeeka was nowhere in sight. At that moment, I didn't care that I hurt her feelings. She should have never even joked with me like that. All three of their asses knew how I felt about Wakeem, so to play like that was never gone make me laugh. I got my lunch and proceeded to our regular table. I wasted no time digging into the partially hot food. I was eating like I hadn't ate all day but I really hadn't eaten since last night when my grandma brought us Chinese, so this food was right on time. Bryson joined me at the table with no sign of Onisha or Javeeka.

"Where they asses at?" I said through a mouth full of chicken parm.

"Javeeka in the bathroom crying chiii. So, Neeka went to check on her," Bryson said nonchalantly, biting into his chicken sandwich. I rolled my eyes at the idea of Onisha babying Javeeka. I continued eating as me and Bryson shared light conversation until it was time for us to head to our media class. Javeeka and Onisha had a separate class from us so this lil fit that Javeeka was in would probably last for the rest of the day. As I gathered my tray and headed for the trash receptacles, I felt a hard bump as my leftover remnants splatter up on my shirt. My eyes locked with Patrice's. She continued walking with her raggedy friends as she left me with a mess all over my light pink Ralph Lauren polo shirt. To say I was pissed was an understatement. I wanted to beat the dog shit out of this girl simply off principle, but I had too many infractions to touch her and my grandma would kick my ass worst if I had her out at this school one more time. Bryson stood off to the side, giving Patrice the death stare to the back of her head as she and her friends exited the cafeteria.

"Ooooh Bitch! I wish I was a girl so I could hit that bitch one good time," he said as he did a quick one-two combo.

I laughed and shook my head at his antics as we too headed out the door to our class. This day couldn't get any worse but when I saw our school's resource officer standing with Patrice and friends in tow, I knew shit was about to get worse.

Bryson stood next to me as the resource officer took hold of my wrist and pulled back my jacket, exposing Patrice's watch on my wrist.

"Told you best friend! She had it!" one of her friends exclaimed. I forgot the girl doing the most had the same gym as us and must have seen me showing it off to my friends. I could kick my own ass right now as the resource officer asked me to remove the watch as he handed it back to Patrice. He placed my now bare wrist in the cuffs he wore on his belt. Bryson looked on with sympathy as I was escorted to the front office to be driven by the same officer to the juvenile detention center. I looked back one last time to see a huge devilish smile etched on Patrice's face. My grandma was going to kill me.

Chapter Eight

-Zai-

Coach B was really working a young nigga in practice and while I didn't mind working a little harder, I was becoming more tired from trying to move packs and balance school and basketball. I wasn't no stellar student or nothing but I did enough to get by. I was trying my hardest to finish my freshman year with at least a C average in most of my classes, but I was failing my English Lit class and I didn't see myself pulling the grade up in time. I was half listening as my U.S. History teacher was trying to explain how a bill became a law for the hundredth time. I was damn near sleep as I fought hard to keep my eyes open. This was my last class of the day and as much as I wanted to go home and crash for a few hours, I couldn't. When the bell finally sounded, I was slow to move. I just wanted to make it to the block, sell out of my pack, and get home. I would usually call one of my big homies to scoop me up--given how tired I was today would have been a perfect day to utilize them.I had waited too long to reach out for a ride, so I took my sweet time walking from school to the block. After I grabbed some wings and fries from Johnny's, I practically smashed the food as I walked to the trap. I must have just needed something to eat because I was feeling energized after that quick meal. I walked up on the porch to regular hood shit. Fiends were being served, money was being made, and niggas was getting high in between time. I hadn't seen Nero in school and lately he had been right underneath Tone. It was like Tone had taken him under his wings to show him the ropes. While we were both in the streets, Nero seemed to be swimming in the streets doing breast strokes while I was trying to get the lifeguard to pull me out the pool.

I dapped up everyone, making my way to where Dash was giving out packs. I wasn't on protege' level and I didn't want the attention. Basketball at the rec center gave me all the fans I didn't want. Dash rarely conversed with any of us; he stayed with his ears glued to his phone as he either argued with his baby mama or he was making moves. He signaled for me to grab the pack closer to edge before he went back to talking on his phone. I found a spot in the living room to bust my pack down, so I could hurry up and get my day over. I was thinking about posting up on the wall today. I wasn't worried about troll and I would be able to get some of my homework done, too. I know it seems like I am one foot in, one foot out on a lot of things that I do. I was trying to still do things that would be pleasing to my mother, regardless of her absence.

Once I had separated my product in small clear baggies, I was headed to post up a few blocks over away from all the extra traffic the trap came with. As I made the short walk over to where the graffiti etched wall sat separating the business from the residential houses, I placed the sacks in the pocket of my hoody as I pulled out my Algebra II book and proceeded to finish the homework, that I had started while in class. What was considered hard for most was easy to me. As I breezed through my math homework, a regular of mine, named Fernando walked up.

"Youngin' lemme get a lil something for my ol' lady. She been trippin' on me," he said as his eyes darted from left to right. His head stayed on a swivel and he often looked out if he seen troll. I reached in my pocket and pulled out the small package that kept his girl, Maria, calm and kept my pockets fat. He slid the money to me in a discreet manner and as quickly as he appeared, he was headed back down the sidewalk headed to his crib. I took the free time I had to pull out my history book to start my paper about the Harlem Renaissance. The material, while it was extensive in providing information, it was actually interesting and had me sucked in. Between reading about musical and art influences during the era the fashion really caught my eyes. The shit reminded me of the movie *Life* and how Ray and

Claude dressed. I was so immersed in gathering this information that I hadn't realized how much of my paper I had wrote already. Despite feeling tired, seeing how much I had accomplished on the assignment made me strive to finish the rest. It was a rare occasion that I even turned in work, but this topic was not only interesting it showed Black people in a positive light. I was more than happy to turn this in. As I finished the two-page paper, my day sped up as I quickly sold out of the rest of my work and headed home to finally get some much-needed rest.

Chapter Nine

-Destiny-

My grandmother had been cussin' Desire ass out since she had to leave her job to pick her up from JDC. I had been pretending like I was listening to music the entire ride. I didn't feel bad for my sister, her lil klepto ass needed to learn a hard lesson. She had been crying hysterically since they released her lil ass. I was trying so hard not to let a smile come across my face. I had been warning her ass to stop trying to be a hot girl with her lil friends but now her ass was in the backseat of our grandma's car, damn near hyperventilating.

"I told yo lil ass if I had to leave my damn job one mo mu'fuckin time, I was gone beat yo ass Desire! Didn't I?" my grandma yelled as she angrily weaved in and out of traffic.

I know you hear me lil girl. You think you fuckin grown?" my grandma questioned Desire while she stared at her through the rearview mirror.

"N.. noo…" Desire managed to get out before she was interrupted by a hard sniffle she couldn't control if she tried. I was fighting so hard not to bust out laughing, this shit was gold. At this moment, her ass knew she was a child and had acted just as a child would had they gotten in trouble.

"You must think you do! Do you know how much that fuckin watch you decided to take, cost? Don't even answer that, I know yo ass couldn't afford it! But you about to cash this check yo thieving ass decided to cash. I'ma beat the breaks off yo lil ass when we get home."

I sat and listened as my sister started crying harder. This wasn't her first time being in trouble for stealing but it was her first time getting put in JDC. If my grandma said she was gone beat us, she was going to do just that. As we got closer to home, Desire was in the back trying to act like she had fallen asleep. I knew that trick all too well, hell I had taught it to her ass. It might have worked on our mama when we were little, but our grandma could see through the bullshit. She whipped into our driveway so fast that Desire's ass flew to the other side of the car. If she thought she could play sleep, our grandma's reckless driving had just woken that ass up. I was the first out the car with my key in hand. I knew my grandma wasn't gonna let Desire make it to the room before she laid hands on her lil ass. I hurried inside as I prepared for the showdown that was moments from happening. I could still hear my grandma going in as the door finally opened and they entered.

Grandma Bev didn't even let Desire make it good into the house before the leather belt that hung from the entryway closet was wrapped firmly around her hand and she was swinging it at her ass. Desire was hollering and trying to avoid getting hit, but our grandma was wildly swinging the belt and grabbing the hand Desire was trying to use to avoid being hit. I was just standing in the hallway, watching as every hit connected.

"Didn't I tell yo lil ass if I had to come down to that damn school one mo mu'fuckin time, I was gone lay hands on yo ass!" our grandma said between every word as she hit Desire with the thick ass belt. I was kinda starting to feel bad for her. Desire was looking at me with tears streaming down her face with pleading eyes. I wish I could have helped her. I thought talking to her as her big sister was helping, but Desire just didn't listen. As I heard the belt moved through the air, you could hear it coming down on her. What had once been me basking in her finally getting chastised had turned into empathy because our grandma was going in. I couldn't watch this ass whoopin' anymore. As I retreated to my room, I felt a wave of nausea hit me. I picked up the pace as I hurried to the bathroom Desire and I shared. I barely made it to the toilet as the contents of my stomach spilled into the toilet.

As I hugged the toilet, my eyes were tear-filled and I couldn't figure out why I would be throwing up. I had only eaten a light lunch in between my classes today and I wasn't really hungry after. I waited for the wave of sickness to pass before getting off my knees. I looked at my now swollen eyes in the mirror and splashed water on my face. I felt another wave of sickness coming, so I bent back over the toilet as I dry heaved and then more stomach acid poured out. I spent the next fifteen minutes trying to regain my composure. I decided to take a hot shower and brush my teeth in hopes that the hot water and a fresh mouth would aid in me feeling better. I wrapped up in my cheetah print bathrobe and headed towards my room. I had to walk past Desire's room to get to mine. Her door was partially cracked, and I could see her in the room crying and talking. I peeked in more and she was talking to a picture of our mom and dad together.

"Momma why you left us? I miss ya'll," she said through her tears. She stared down at the pictures as her tears fell on the glass. I quietly backed away from her door with my own set of fresh tears. I missed them too and hated seeing my little sister like that. I made it to my room and got into bed and drifted off to sleep with my parents on my mind.

The Next Day

I woke up sick again and finally realized that I went to bed without eating. I was feeling fatigued and like I could throw up again. Thank God it was Saturday because I planned on just lying in my bed and not moving. As I planned my day to just lounge, my Grandma Bev walked into my room without knocking.

"Getcho ass up girl ain't nobody chillin' today. You and yo bad ass sister going down to the community center and ya'll joining one of them damn programs. Ya'll ain't finna be laid up in my shit doing nothing," she said as she yanked back the curtains in my room and opened the blinds.

I was trying not to let the huff I was holding in escape; that would have just fueled her fire. I threw the covers off of me and delayed rising too fast because of how I was feeling. I also didn't want to alarm her of my current condition. She exited out of my room as quick as she had entered, and I stretched before throwing my feet over the bed and standing up. Desire was coming out of the bathroom as I was heading into it. She still looked down about yesterday and didn't say much as she tied up her poetic braids into a bun on top of her head and went back to her room. I quickly did my hygiene routine, trying my hardest to ignore the feeling I was feeling. I ran into my grandmother as she headed towards the front door.

"You taking us to the rec, right?" I asked, tying my hair in a low ponytail. I still needed to throw on some clothes but my grandma digging in her purse and looking up at me let me know that we were going to have to get ourselves there.

"Now you know ya'll asses can walk to that damn rec. I ain't wasting my damn gas to go round the corner. But you better get there, Coach B gone tell me if ya'll asses there or not," she said before locating whatever she was looking for in her bag and walking out the door. The huff I had been holding in, finally expelled out of my body as I involuntarily rolled my eyes and headed in my room to put on some clothes.

As I finished adjusting the vertical striped romper from Romwe, Desire was knocking on my door before poking her head in.

"You almost ready to go?" she asked with a slight attitude

"Um yeah, let me grab my fanny pack, and then we can go," I replied with a matching tone.

She rolled her eyes before closing my door. I sighed and grabbed my phone, lip gloss, keys and some money before exiting my room and meeting an already annoyed Desire at the door.

"Man fix your face I'on wanna go to this shit either but yo ass the reason we gotta even go," I said with an attitude as I locked the door and started walking ahead of her. Desire was dragging behind me as we made our way up the three blocks it took to get to the rec center. I spotted Tone's red Jag on gold twenty-eight-inch rims as it rides past us with the music blasting from behind the tinted windows. I needed a nigga like that with ends and one day I was going to find me a nigga that was papered up to call my own. I was still fantasizing about my future rich thug when my feet hit the asphalt that lead to the rec center off the street. When I looked up, Nero was hopping out of Tone's nice car and walking up to Zai. I watched as they dapped each other up with Nero pointing in our direction. Desire's mood seemed to brighten the closer we got to the boys. The one that was behind me the whole way here was now in front of me, making strides to get over to where they were standing. Her bad ass was probably trying to solidify her spot in the smoke session that was bound to commence later.

"Cousins!" Desire greeted them as if she hadn't just been in the worst mood ever. I rolled my eyes at her sudden change of attitude as I walked up and gave both Zai and Nero hugs. We all walked inside the rec center together.

"So ya'll back at the rec for good?" Zai asked as he sat down to readjust his laces on his basketball shoes.

"We only here cause ya'll lil cousin here, got her ass whooped yesterday, done got caught stealing somebody's Apple watch and shit," I said, cutting my eyes at Desire, who sucks her teeth at my statement before trying to defend herself.

"First of all, shut up Destiny. I ain't get caught doing nothing. Somebody snitched on me," she said with her attitude resurfacing quickly.

"Cousin it sounds like to me yo ass got caught stealing," Zai said with a smirk as she rolled her eyes his way next. Dinero is all in his phone with his fingers moving effortlessly and quickly on his touch screen. He finally slides his phone in his pocket before engaging in the conversation.

"Cousin what the hell I told you about taking people shit. That shit could get you messed up out in these streets," he argued with so much seriousness behind his words. Zai and I nodded our heads to agree with his statement.

Desire thought the shit was a game and while we hated what happened to our parents, it was that very thing that ultimately got them killed. It was as if what Nero had just said had Desire thinking, but I knew she wouldn't be taking anything from it. It was like she heard it, but it went in one ear and out the other. Even though she was ten, Desire was mature for her age and often times it was hard remembering that about her, or any of us for that matter. We chopped it up with the boys for a few more minutes before they left us sitting at the glass bulletin board, looking over the list of programs they offered. I knew Zai came to practice faithfully but Nero had missed more than a few practices and games. I wouldn't be surprised if Coach B kicked him off the team for his absence. I scrolled through the programs list and Coach B had expanded more since the last time I had been here. It had only been cheerleading when I started out and pottery but now the list was extensive; quite a few of the programs stood out like the MUA program or the scrapbooking program. Both of those drew me in, but I was definitely interested in the make-up one. Desire was acting like she was looking at the list, but you could tell she couldn't have cared less.

"You see anything you like?" I asked, trying to see what she was leaning towards.

"No!" she snapped at me with an eye roll to accompany her brash tone. I shook my head and walked off towards the front desk that housed the sign-up sheets. I smiled at the lady at the desk and grabbed one of the clipboards and found a seat to sign-up. Desire was still standing at the bulletin board, acting like she was mad at the world when a boy no older than her stopped in front of her. The scowl she wore quickly dissolved into a genuine coy smile. She liked him; I could tell. I watched their interaction for a few more seconds before turning my attention back to the form in front of me. When I looked back up, the boy was giving my sister a hug and heading back to the gym. She watched him walk away with a smile on her face. She looked up at the board again this time with interest and ran her fingers down the list of programs. She practically ran over to the desk to grab a clipboard. As I rose to turn my form in, the same feeling I had experienced the night before came over me and I was running towards the nearest restroom.

Thankfully, the bathroom was empty when I rushed in and I immediately went into the first stall I came to. I stood over the toilet as my stomach went through waves of convulsions. My stomach was empty but managed to produce something that was forcing me to gag and release the contents into the toilet. I was feeling weak with every attempt to feel better. I heard the bathroom door open, but no one said anything. I could hear the sink in the bathroom running but still no one said anything as I fought with myself to regain control of my body. I had tears coming down my face as I finally felt the nauseating feeling subside. When I finally unlatched the bathroom door, the lady from the front desk of the rec center was standing there with a wet paper towel and a cup of water. I looked up at her with tears still lingering in my eyes as I took the paper towel and dabbed at my heated brow area. I felt horrible. I took the cup from her next and sipped on the room temperature water. It felt good going down my now raw throat.

"Thank you," I finally said as she just stared at me with a weird look. The way she was staring at me had me thinking I had vomit or something on my face, so I looked in the mirror.

"How far along are you?" she asked as she played with her fingers that were now resting in front of her.

"Huh? What do you mean how far along am I?" I inquired.

"Honey, you're pregnant. It doesn't take a rocket scientist to see that."

Her revelation about why I was feeling the way I was feeling, took over me. I was in shock, what the hell was I going to do with a baby?

"What's your name, sweetie? I'm Mia," she said, extending her hand for me to shake.

I just looked at her before my feelings and emotions got the best of me and I passed out.

Chapter Ten

-Bandy-

"That's how you do it, Waka!" I yelled with excitement as Wakeem scrimmaged against his other teammates. We had a game this upcoming Saturday and the boys were looking sharp. Even Nero was out on the court playing like he had been coming to practice. I was pissed when he strolled his ass in my practice today like he had been a part of what these boys had been building as a team. My brother's call earlier about the pressure Dinero was putting on these nigga's necks out in these streets made me let jit practice even if I knew I had no intentions of letting his ass play in one game. His ass was supposed to follow behind Zaire and get so wrapped up in basketball--or one of the other sports I offered here--that the street shit wouldn't even happen. Both boys sadly had fallen weak to the fabricated facade that the street life promoted and glorified.

While I didn't condone their life choices, my own personal involvement had me hella guilty for them even having to jump off the porch. My own conscience was eating the fuck away at me. Dash told me he caught both they asses hanging at our trap spot the youngins came to make money at. He hit my line up soon as he sent their asses on their way empty-handed. After I did my own digging up on their living situations, I ok'd them making money in the spot. They were eleven at the time and while they were far too young to be doing what I allowed them to do, it was only gonna fly if me, and my brother, and Dash kept an eye on them. We each promised not to get attached to any of them and for the past few years it had worked without any of us showing any of them special attention. But life has a funny way of connecting people to you and while I knew why I could never be too far from any of them, I obviously took a liking to the boys and Zaire in particular because he had been Shadequa's son.

Every kid that came to this rec center knew me as Coach B. They knew me from this motivation-filled, unconditional loved environment that my staff and I provided. As a kid growing up, I was in an unloved and often lonely environment. I recognized the need for a safe haven; especially for black kids. Not to say non-black kids didn't need their own safe havens too, but my black ass was born with two strikes against me at birth. There was a desperate need for a safe place that kids going through my similar upbringing needed. I had been arrested a total of forty-seven times before my eighteenth birthday and that was after juvenile no longer wanted to handle my cases after I turned sixteen. Every second chance, alternative school, or program you could think of, I had been to. If there was a Netflix documentary about black youth in the Florida correctional facilities in the mid 2000's, I would have been one of the poster children for the show. Despite my parent's being not worth a damn for me or my brother, it was only right I got off my ass at fifteen and made something really shake. If I didn't hustle for myself, I did so for my lil brother, Tone, until he could do it for himself. Selling dope was easy, it was the other shit that came with doing it.

My father had been a kingpin on the rise turned baser, who treated his nose with cocaine until he was found dead from an apparent cocaine overdose when I was ten. Him and our mother, Loretta, had been neighborhood sweethearts even with strict orders from my grandparents to steer clear of my daddy and any man like him. My mother apparently wanted something different from the quiet girl role she had been accustomed to. She hadn't listened to my granddad when she had been forbidden from being with my dad only to end up pregnant not once but twice by him. My grandpops was a city council member for the city of St. Pete. He was a very prominent man in the black community. My grandfather sat alongside some of the most powerful men to ever make significant changes for our community. So for his only daughter to basically become the live-in whore to one of the biggest dope boys in the hood at the time, that shit rattled not only my grandpops feathers but a few black city officials. My father had my mother looking crazy as fuck out in these streets and I had lived through a lot of shit they had done to each other and us. I had seen a lot in our two-bedroom house that no kid should have been subjected to. My upbringing had led me directly down the incorrect path of my own undoing.

Even though he never said it, my grandfather Hasan Daniels, hated my father. I believe it was the sheer fact that he had subjected my mother to a life that was beneath her. He had always spoiled my mother; she was the quintessential example of a daddy's girl. My grandfather must have hated that my mother had fallen for my dad's smooth talking and flashy money. For the life of me, I couldn't understand why my mama would leave the comfortable folds of her cushy life to be with someone like my pops. That nigga obviously didn't care about her because had it been me, I would have been telling my lady to stay in school and get to her mu'fuckin bag. Had I been my granddad, I would have been ten toes down in the paint for my daughter. Hell, he had raised and showed her how a man should treat her and instead of grasping the lesson, she chased this sheltered girl's dream of a guy from the hood that ended up being nothing more than a junkie.

I could recall Mom's and grandpops got in this really heated fight when I was seven. I remember being so happy because I knew my grandparents were going to have gifts for me when they came over to see us. The whole day, my mama primped and primed our small home for their visit, and she had even talked my daddy into getting us all something to wear for the occasion. When my father ruined dinner by being more than two hours late, and then he disrespected my mother right in front of her own father. He ended the night by calling my granddad a cracker ass kisser straight to his face. My grandpops practically drug my grandmother out of our house after my mother took up for my dad in the situation. That was the last time I saw my grandad until I was ten. And we were burying my father then, and mama had to call her parents for that.

Tone or Antone is six years younger than me. From the moment that nigga could say my name, he had been following behind me. So when the infamous Antonio Wright was found by one of his runners face down in his own product, it didn't take a rocket scientist to figure out what happened. He died from breaking the cardinal rule when it came to being a dealer: "Don't get high off your own supply." At ten and four we were fatherless, and our mother had become mindless and stuck with two black boys. I was getting in trouble every turn I took. I had been getting in trouble well before my father even died. I loved the streets too much to ever leave or so I thought.

When I got my third charge for possession and after my dad had drug my mother through the mud for the last time, my grandfather came to try and get a grip on us all but it was too late. While our grandfather spoiled me and my brother, he was still a strict disciplinarian when it came to showing us how to be men. Our father had dropped the ball there and Grandpa Hasan was doing anything to prevent us from being just like him or worst.

The last time my grandfather got a phone call from one of his buddies down at SPPD, he came to get my black ass out and damn near killed my ass from drilling his philosophies in my head. Eventually something clicked and I was feeling what my grandfather was saying. The bullshit my father had taught me was deliberately and skillfully reprogrammed out of my thought process. It had been executed by my grandfather effortlessly. I still was able to rise in the streets while being mentored on how to be a real man. Even though I still was in the streets, I had applied the shit I was learning from my grandpops. He helped change me into a business-minded young man. While having my own drug company, unbeknownst to my grandpa, I was meeting the grandsons and granddaughters to some of St. Pete's black elite. I was networking my ass off back then.

I wanted to invest my dirty money into something that could be here long after I was gone. It had been a small dream to give something back to my community once my money was right. Spending all that time with my grandpa had turned my ass into a hood philanthropist. I had envisioned this place where kids could escape from their problems and receive what they weren't getting at home. At the time when I was just going over the official blueprint for this place. I had no idea that my dreams would finally come true when I broke ground on this place. As I watched my boys finish their scrimmage amongst one another. I thought back to the day my life decided to align.

Chapter Eleven

-Desire-

This morning I was loathing the idea of going to the rec center. I was pissed that Patrice's raggedy friend had been hating hard on me. My grandma had my phone, which equaled my life. I cried like a whole bitch yesterday when my grandma whooped me but what did ya'll expect? I'm ten years old for crying out loud. Mix that with being born a girl and you had the right recipe for instant tears. I had been getting whooped by my grandma since about four, so I knew the type of ass whoopins my grandma dished out. I had watched her whoopins evolved from teachable moments to the 'she didn't give no fucks' beatings. "Today's welts were from yesterday's decisions," she use to say back when she was actin' all godly. She would do the most whoopin us; her over-the-top ways would have you thinking if you wanted to risk the trouble. Even though we got disciplined when it was necessary--for the most part--she gave a lot of chances along the way, accompanied with a bunch of empty threats she'd just yell and threaten to stomp a hole in ya ass. Then dared you to say anything else to her. Yesterday had been overkill in my opinion.

I didn't deserve all of that, she had taken out some of her outside aggression. I couldn't have been the reason for all that force that was behind the whoopin I received yesterday. I went to sleep last night feeling lost and I missed my parents terribly. I had only spent four years with them. I knew them, but I barely knew them. Just like they barely knew me when they left. I had gone to sleep angry, sad, and still a little freaked out by the detention center. Yeah, I was cool with people who stayed in and out of JDC and other juvenile programs, but this was my first time being there. It was a whole other world and if it was emulating what big jail was, then I was good on that whole scenario. I wasn't built for none of those officers yelling and spitting in my direction. I didn't like how they were talking to me in there and I'd do what I needed, to never step foot in there again. It was beneath me.

This morning had been a blur. I just remembered being told by my Grandma Bev, how I was going to the rec today. Since I was still not talking to her, I refused to respond to her after the way she handled me last night. If I recall correctly, she had mumbled something about my daddy just having to breed with that girl. As if my mother was below her trifflin' ass son or something. In my little eyes back then, they were equal. Don't get me wrong, I loved my daddy when he was alive. He spoiled us but talked so much crap about my mama when he would have us. My grandma, too. They talked a whole lotta shit about my mama, it had me and my sister paying attention to how we were being raised. While she could have done better, she made sure we were straight. I missed both of them and I wished the person who took them from me was dead, too. I purposely walked slower behind Destiny this morning because I knew that would piss her off. After catching her wanting to laugh at my pain and suffering due to our grandma, that bitch could eat rocks. I was so glad to see Dinero at the center. It was a rarity to even catch him anywhere away from the block.

When both he and Zai started going in on me, I was done listening to any of them. They thought because I was the youngest that I was too young to be doing some of the things I was into but the last I checked, they too were engaged in activities not fit for kids their ages. So, if anyone was asking me my opinion, everyone should have just minded their own fuckin' business and let me do me. Ten or not, I was going to take what I liked and now getting caught just drove me to not get caught the next time. I wouldn't show off one thing I snatched from here on out. I wasn't involving none of my so-called friends in my business and I damn sure wasn't helping no one take shit. I was going solo on my five-finger discounting. When

Destiny finally moved her bobble head ass away from the board that listed the available choices, I was still uninterested but running into Wakeem ignited the interest I needed, just so I could see him. Javeeka's lil comment, even though I know in my heart she was playing, I bet she learned a valuable lesson about playing with me. I still hadn't heard from her or anyone else that claimed to be my friend but shit, I guess they really couldn't with Beverly confiscating my phone. I settled on a program that I felt would suit me as I made my way to the desk to grab my own clipboard. The receptionist lady smiled at me briefly and then went back to whatever it was she was doing. I wasn't even halfway done filling out the program form before I caught a quick glance of my sister bolting for the bathroom. A few moments later, the same receptionist calmly walked in behind her. I shrugged off the occurrence and finished filling out my sheet. When I sat the clipboard and pen back on the desk, the same woman came out of the bathroom in a rush with panic etched across her face. My heart dropped to the pit of my small stomach. I knew it was Destiny.

"Someone call 911!" she belted out. The other receptionist picked up the phone almost immediately as she followed her request. I took off near the bathroom; if something was wrong, I needed to be there for her. The lady that had been in here with her had to have gone to get Coach B. I found Destiny sprawled about on the bathroom floor. She didn't physically look hurt, she looked sleep a little. She was breathing, I could see her chest rising and falling but she wasn't responding to anything I was saying to her. I even lightly tapped her face, seeing as I knew she hated for anyone to play in her face. She still didn't move, and I was getting worried. When the same receptionist came in with EMTs behind her, she and I moved out of the way as they tried assessing Destiny's current prognosis. Within minutes, they had her strapped to the gurney and headed out to the ambulance. I walked out of the bathroom, visibly shook. My cousins ran over to me and started firing off questions, but I couldn't find the words necessary to answer them. I was just in a daze. Trying to make sense of everything going on around me.

Chapter Twelve

-Dinero-

After listening to all the praises Waka and Zai had gotten from Coach, I knew he wasn't checking for my black ass. He and everyone else on this team knew I had natural born baller skills. He was just letting a nigga exercise if you asked me. Tone had told him how I had been handling shit in the streets and he probably just wanted to see a nigga hoop for old time's sake. I really didn't want to come down here, but Tone insisted so I obliged the OG. I wasn't into this kid shit no more and I had no desire to go pro. I'd leave that shit to Zaire. I knew my surrogate cousin wasn't trying to obtain street fame and while basketball wasn't his shit before, he had perfected his shit and now cuz was ballin'. He had even managed to shake me a couple times on the court, but I never let that nigga know he had surprised me with his new skill set. I hadn't expected to see the girls here either but after Desire's lil ass got caught stealing, I knew Grandma Bev wasn't going to let that shit ride too long without making them do something more constructive with their time, especially Desire. I was glad I got to see they ass; I was always grindin' and barely had time for myself. I hadn't seen them since we had dinner the other night and we preferred keeping them as far from the trap as we could but that was easier said than done. Coach B was giving out instructions for an upcoming game they had, and I was off to the side checking my phones. I had a few weed drop-offs in the hood as well as a coke sell that I had been waiting on since before Tone scooped me up.

I was in the middle of replying to a text from my lil boo on my main phone, when the fine ass receptionist came in nearly running, completely negating the fact that Coach B was talking. She walked up on him so quick and whispered in his ear. The expression that was on his face when she just busted in had turned from disapproval to sheer fear. Everyone caught on to the sudden change as he followed behind her, which prompted all of us to follow behind them to see what was up. I caught up to Zai as we both made our way to the main lobby where EMTs were wheeling someone out on a stretcher.

"Man, that looked like Destiny," he said, rubbing the back of his neck. I wasn't sure it was until Desire's body came into my direct view as she stood off to the side of the bathroom. I tapped Zai and made a gesture towards Desire, who looked out of it. I knew then that the person they had just wheeled out was in fact Destiny. Zai and I started firing off question after question at Desire, but she never answered us. It was like she had gone mute. Her eyes were blinking but she was somewhere else. I saw Coach B talking to the fine lady who had just interrupted his pep talk and I could see that they were quite familiar with one another, but I couldn't care less who Coach B was familiar with. I wanted to see how my cousin was doing. By the time Tone strolled into the lobby, most of the other kids and parents had vacated and Coach B said something to him in his ear. I didn't know how they knew one another but Coach B kept his ears to the streets. I had never seen him come to any of the dope spots or anything that remotely hinted at him having his feet in the game, but Tone kept himself around Coach B. I couldn't put my finger on their connection, but I wasn't going to worry about how well they knew each other.

Tone could see me approaching them and I saw his lips moving but couldn't make out what he had said.

"Yo Nero, you ready to peel out young blood?" Tone asked with a slight smile.

"Umm yeah but I wanna go check on my cousin first." Tone looked at Coach B like he needed permission from the nigga or something. I was paying attention to their weird interaction when I felt Zai walk up with Desire.

"Coach B can you take us to the hospital to check on Destiny? They grandma not picking up," Zai informed Coach B. Tone looked at his phone and then back at Coach B before Coach B said anything. It was as if he didn't want to, but he knew he had to. If they were going to see Destiny, I was riding too. There was no way I wasn't going. I spoke up this time.

"Aye Coach if you taking them, I'm coming too." I wasn't asking, I was telling him.

He knew that already as a small sigh escaped his body. I watched him walk over to the same receptionist and whisper in her ear before watching her nod her head and return back to work. He walked back over to us and dapped Tone up before leading us out to his black-on-black 2018 Genesis G80. We only had seconds to admire the vehicle as Zai and Desire got in the back and I hopped up front with Coach B. As soon as he cranked up the car, Derez De'Shon's voice filled the insides with *P.I.L* playing. Listening to the lyrics had me mentally making a note to go check out more of this nigga's songs. I could relate to the shit he was talking about. I let the words of the lyrics get me from the rec to All Children's Hospital, where Destiny had been transported. It was a Wednesday, so traffic was moderate as Coach B navigated through St. Pete traffic. It was nearly eight in the evening and we were getting through every light that we were coming to. Fifteen minutes of standard city traffic and we were pulling into the visitor parking lot as Coach B led the way to the emergency entrance.

When we walked in, the emergency room wasn't crowded at all. It was a few people sitting with sick kids, but it didn't seem like we would be waiting long.

"Ya'll have a seat, let me go see what's going on," Coach B instructed us before walking over to the admissions desk. As he engaged in conversation with the receptionist, I pulled out my phone and responded to my boo and shot Tone a text, letting him know I wouldn't be hitting the block tonight. I never took breaks but from the looks of today's events, I knew Desire wouldn't want to be alone and knowing that Grandma Bev wasn't picking up her phone just meant Desire would have to fend for herself tonight. At least she wouldn't be alone, at least I knew I was going to be there to keep her company. We were all we had, and I refused to leave my lil cousin home alone without someone there. It was like Zai was in my brain because he said,

"I'on know where ya'll grandma at but I'll stay at the house with you, Desire." She gave him a smile as she fumbled with her fingers in her lap.

"Hell, me too. We ain't finna let you thug in that house by yourself. I already let it be known I'm in for the night," I proudly stated. Zai looked over at me with a smile on his face as well. Regardless of where life pulled any of us, we knew we had to have one another's backs. It was our destiny to be with each other for life or at least it felt like it. We all observed Coach B walking back over to us as we all anticipated what he said next.

"So ya'll asses can't go to the back to see her, it's hospital policy," he continued before any of us could protest, "I'm going in the back to see what's what and then I'll be able to give ya'll the real. If they will let her go home with us is still unknown, but I'll know more once I get from back there. Here, go grab ya'll some shit out the vending machines or something. I'll be back soon," he said, giving us a twenty-dollar bill before walking off towards the double doors that led to the back and disappearing behind the automatic locked doors.

While Coach B was in the back, it felt like we had been out in the waiting room for hours but each time I checked my phone it had only been minutes. Zai had given his phone to Desire so she could check her social media accounts. Grandma Bev had to have been really pissed to take her phone, but I knew she meant business if she hadn't given it back before she left. Zai was reading one of the health magazines they had spread on one of their tables and this nigga looked like he was actually into it. I wanted to clown this nigga but the nudes my lil boo had just sent me had all my attention. I must have been wearing my expression because when I looked up from my phone, Zai was looking at me all crazy.

"Damn cuz whatever you looking at, got you making them faces Trey Songz be making when he singing to these females," he clowned.

I waved him off as I sent the purple eggplant emoji with the water droplet one. If Destiny was straight, I might have had to make a pit stop before heading in for the night. We waited for what seemed like forever. Desire was now leaning up on the side of Zai, knocked out as he watched basketball highlights on YouTube. I had since semi-promised my lil boo thang, that I was going to slide through her peoples' spot to put it in her life. I knew how I was, so there was no telling where I could end up if we didn't have to stay with Desire for the night. Hell, just sitting here was starting to make me tired. I yawned my hardest yawn as

Coach B finally came from the back. I didn't think Coach B was close to forty but the look he wore suggested he had just aged in rocket speed.

"Come on ya'll." He didn't say anything else to us until we were all back in his car. Desire, who had been dead asleep, was now wide awake from having to walk to the car. She was the first to say something.

"Coach B, is my sister alright?" Desire asked genuinely. We all wanted to know. Given we were now headed towards Central Ave towards our neighborhood suggested things might be more serious than we all thought. Coach B was sitting in the driver seat with his eyes straight on the road.

"Desire, I think you need to talk to your grandma about your sister. It's not my place to disclose her current state to any of you. I know she's ok for now, but I called your grandma before leaving your sister and she spoke to both of us. I am dropping you off and they will see you shortly. Boys, where am I dropping ya'll off at?" he asked, still never taking his eyes off the road. I couldn't tell if he was mad, upset, or just being him. It was weird, I could definitely tell he was thinking though.

"I'ma stay with Desire until her grandma get home," Zai spoke up.

"Yeah me too, Coach," I added.

Nothing else was said the rest of the way. Once Coach B's car had turned the corner and Desire finally let us in, we got good and comfortable on Grandma Bev's Haverty's navy blue sectional. We all had our own lil section of the couch and while I knew I had made plans, the lack of sleep I had been experiencing took over me and I was slumped.

Chapter Thirteen

-Zai-

"Ya'll be glad ya'll boys, Dinero, cause ya lil fast ass cousin here done gone and got her ass pregnant," Grandma Bev said with venom laced in her words.

I couldn't see them, but I could hear them, well her because Nero wasn't saying shit. I woke up in the same position I was in when I sat down. I could feel the crook in my neck as I rose off the couch to stretch. I lowkey didn't even want to make my presence known because Grandma Bev had a way of dragging a conversation. Hearing that Destiny was pregnant wasn't a surprise to me. I knew enough about my surrogate cousin to know how she got down. I just hoped whatever bum ass nigga she let blow her up was going to step up, otherwise me and Nero had no problem beating him down before taking responsibility of the unknown being.

I drug my feet underneath me as I made my way around the corner. Destiny, Nero, and Grandma Bev were all in the kitchen. Destiny looked like she had the weight of the world on her shoulders and Nero looked like he was ready to get out of Grandma Bev's ranting path. Hell, I barely wanted to wake up to it, so I knew he had been listening much longer and was beyond ready to slide.

"Zaire look atcha looking like your damn mama," Bev said, taking a swig from her coffee mug.

I gave her a quick smile and made direct eye contact with Nero. He had the look of 'help me, nigga' etched across his face. I wanted to chuckle aloud, but I didn't want to receive a nasty look from Grandma Bev. You didn't want to get this woman going, she didn't know how to let shit go. I'm sure Destiny was going through it right now with her telling us about it all out in the house. Desire still wasn't up and I'm sure if she wasn't, she would be with the way they grandma was carrying on.

"Zaire and Dinero, ya'll know if you round here sticking ya'll lil peedawacker's in these lil girls like ya cousin, she said, cutting her eyes and staring intensely at Destiny, whose head hadn't rose since I had been in the kitchen. "You could be somebody damn daddy round here," she said, locking her eyes on me and then shifting her gaze Nero's way. I shifted on my feet, feeling the energy change drastically in the room. Nero's phone started going off like it was on cue. He ran over to Grandma Bev and kissed her on the cheek before telling her, him and I had to run. Her response was a "Mhm." Before she could say anything else,

I turned on my heels, stepped into my Air Max 95's, and snatched my phone and wallet off the table. I wouldn't normally leave without going to show Grandma Bev some love but today she was on one or more and I didn't have the time for it. As we were heading out the door, Desire was walking out her room rubbing her eyes. She would be mad she wiped that sleep out her eyes once her grandma started going in.

We walked the short walk to the block. I was scrolling my phone looking at all my notifications. Nero was in his phone too, laughing at dumb ass videos and responding to his buddies. We had literally spent the entire night in last night and lord knows Nero didn't just sit for anyone. We had vowed at their funerals that we would never flake on one another, we would be ride or die just like our parents. That shit was from the cradle to the grave for us and last night Desire needed us. I caught up with everything just as we rounded the corner approaching the block. It was nine thirty in the morning and the block was already jumpin'.

Junkies were already at the backdoor asking for a wake-up. It was like us young niggas were selling Folgers to these fiends and they came back faithfully. I was intrigued by the money but Coach B's added pressure to hone in on my basketball skills were starting to pay off. I was starting to see the growth and it was motivating me to look into pursuing this further than the rec. Wakeem was only eleven and that lil nigga was a savage on the court, he was a great teammate and competitor to spar with. I had begun to evolve more into an athlete and was using my last year on the community center's team to train for my freshman year on JV. While I was clearly ready for Varsity, the school wouldn't allow freshmen to join varsity until their sophomore year. I wasn't sweating that shit. I would use JV as a way to gain fans since the crowd would be more than just people out the neighborhood. I would possibly gain some national love if people did the norm and recorded me playing. I would definitely catch somebody's eye in the sports world.

We neared the porch as we dapped up everybody. Tone and Dash could be heard inside, arguing amongst one another when we hit the door. We could tell their game of 2K had turned for the worst.

"Nigga why you over there cheatin'," Dash accused as he frantically pressed the buttons on the PS4 controller. Tone was trying his best to ignore him but once he heard cheatin' he went in. Nero and I plopped a seat on the nearby loveseat. Nero pulled a bag of Girl Scout Cookie out of his pocket and a natural and began to roll up. As Tone and

Dash continued to argue over who was doing what to cheat, I was growing tired of the activity at the trap. If this was how our day was starting, I was starting to be over all this shit. I would have to tell my cousin who was more like my brother first. Nero would have to be alright with my decision, all this shit was getting old to me quick.

Chapter Fourteen

-Bandy-

Last night seemed unreal but not unbelievable. I had never had a kid get hurt, slip, or let alone faint in my facility yet last night, Destiny had given me a first. I was aware that Mia had brought her fine ass to work and she ignored me all day. When she had to come tell me about Destiny fainting, she looked genuinely concerned for Destiny's well-being. Any anger she was trying to show was nonexistent at that moment. I had been trying to get her to come home but after the fourth day, she was still on no-go. I had started to just say fuck it but with the incident happening yesterday, here I was in the kitchen whipping up some Belgium waffles equipped with powdered sugar, fresh strawberries and whipped cream, turkey bacon, egg whites, and avocado slices. The meal was complete with two goblets of pulp free orange juice and a cup of piping hot Chai tea for her. I turned off the stove and grabbed the tray that I had everything on and walked to our room.

Mia slept peacefully in her satin pink teddy. The sunlight that had violated our room was making her skin glow something serious. It was making me want to slide in between or legs and say fuck breakfast. Her natural tresses fell over her face, hiding her beautiful features. She looked so serene. I hated to wake her, but she loved my cooking and once she realized food was involved, she wouldn't dare be mad at me. I placed the tray on our dresser and walked over to her side of the bed and started placing soft calculated kisses over her face. She started to stir as I continued dropping kiss after kiss on her face. Her big doe-like eyes finally popped open and focused on me. She wore an instant scowl on her face and I quickly went and retrieved the tray of food and got in bed next to her. As if on cue, her face morphed into a Cheshire cat grin as she sat up to indulge in the spread before her. The first thing she grabbed was the OJ and a slice of the bacon. I grabbed the remote and turned on the forty-inch tv that was mounted to our bedroom wall. The last station on was my go-to and where the tv usually stayed when Mia wasn't using it. Otherwise a nigga would turn on the tv and some ratchet ass shit would be staring back at a nigga. As ESPN showcased the best plays from the previous nights' games, we ate our breakfast as Mia scrolled through her phone, doing the countless things she did on the mu'fucka.

Last night we hadn't even had sex because she didn't want to. I was cool with that, but I had to taste her. It had been days since I had tasted my favorite flavored ice cream and I had to have her cream on my tongue. Of course, she allowed me to do that, but a nigga had to beat one out in the shower this morning because I had gone to bed with a stiffy. I knew she was still mad about the abortion talk and I didn't fault her for wanting to keep this one. But I was not one to be nobody's daddy. Listening to those nurses disclose that Destiny, who is all of sixteen-years-old and is having her own baby--didn't sit well with me. I knew Mia knew since she was probably going through the same symptoms as Destiny, so them being in that bathroom last night might have just complicated my life more. Like I said, I had never shown any of them more attention than the other. I never wanted my personal to overlap with my past but in some strange case of event's it finally had. As we continued eating, I thought back to the day I decided to reach out to their peoples and insert myself in their lives permanently.

The first shovel hit the untouched dirt, for H. Daniels Recreational Center almost ten months prior and construction was moving at a steady pace. A lot of city officials that had served with my grandpops and knew about my history was against me opening the rec center so close to where drug activity and high-level crimes were seconds from happening. Some of them even tried to stop what I was doing but after I went in front of a special board and explained exactly what I was trying to do with a proper business plan, I was approved to start construction on the site I had paid nearly twenty g's for.

Yes, it was smack dab in the middle of the hood but to me those kids needed something close to home, their parents too. I had gotten the foundation laid down and the framework was nearly done. Next, windows installation then we'd be adding furniture. I had just lost my granddad and that made the rec center's completion that more important. I had spent the entire duration of his stay in the hospital by his side. My brother, who at the time was head-first in street shit, volunteered to spearhead my drug business while I stayed by our grandfather's side. While making my transition to step back from the streets, my brother brought an unwanted omen to me, when his young and dumb ass let four women rob him of the money I had factored in helping me get out the business. Those women single-handedly had done something a nigga had never done; they had successfully robbed me.

It would take me four more months before I'd be officially open for business with him and Dash's fuck up. With everything that happened the first year from the media coverage of the murders, it seemed next to impossible that anyone in the neighborhood would be letting their kids attend the at the time limited program rec center. I started my neighborhood campaign to recruit the families in the community near the brand new rec center I had built in honor of my grandfather; who for many was a staple of the community. I was surprised at the number of people that supported the new building. Quite a few of the older people in the neighborhood knew my granddaddy and respected what he stood for. They had seen where I had come from and what I was trying to do. They were quick to help get their kids and grandkids involved. A lot of the niggas I ran with had even volunteered to help out. I remembered the day each of the kids' grandmothers came to sign them up. The year had truly aged them into true grandmothers. I could see the life sucked out of their eyes. They were taking care of these kids out of necessity, not because they cared.

Ms. Bev had been the first to drop her two granddaughters off. I remember thinking about how much they looked like their parents. It was no denying who they belonged to.

"Dey asses need somewhere to go when I ain't home," Ms. Beverly nonchalantly had spoken the day she came in. Our programs were very scarce for the girls, so it was only dance and cheerleading for them. They lasted all of a year and a half before they stopped coming all together. The

boys had sports and when Ms. Janice came to sign up Nero, he was barely talking and kept a mean mug on his face. Once we toured the gym and he got a ball in his hand, he gravitated towards basketball. Ms. Gladys was way more hands on than the other grandmothers for a while but shortly after Zai signed up for our football program, she stopped coming to volunteer all together.

Mia's voice broke me out of my thoughts as she collected our dishes and headed to the kitchen. I watched her plump ass shake effortlessly as she walked away. I wasn't even good and comfortable in the bed before she returned.

"You didn't hear nothing I said Brodrick, huh?" she said with an apparent attitude. Her hip was popped out with her hand resting comfortably on it as she sucked her lips. Plus, she was using a nigga's government name and she knew I hated that shit.

"Man chill, nah I ain't hear you, repeat that shit."

"I ain't!" she said before walking towards our walk-in closet and sifting through her side of clothes. Here she went with this leaving shit again, we were never able to talk our shit out and I knew her silent treatment had started. I grabbed my phone and started checking my emails, unbothered by her usual behavior. Despite me going to bed horny last night after sucking her pussy dry and I had made us breakfast, she was already with the theatrics and it wasn't even eleven yet. I dove into responding to potential investors in several business ventures I was stepping into and not even Mia was going to stop my productivity. If she wanted to leave, she could leave. She thought I was mad I was sure, but little did she know I was cooler than a pickle and her leaving just meant I'd be beating my meat a little bit longer. She stormed into our attached bathroom and slammed the door. A small chuckle begot me as I shook my head and continued being the entrepreneur that I was. She was not about to ruin my day.

Fifteen minutes later, she was stepping back into the room with nothing but a towel and tip-toeing to the closet to get dressed. She knew better than to dress in front of me with her so-called attitude she was throwing around because she would be fucked and smiling once I got done with her. Before I saw her, I felt her presence re-enter into a usually spacious environment. I was trying hard to ignore her, but her energy was heavy. She stood at the closet's opening as she stared daggers at me. If looks could kill, a nigga would be dead as fuck. I was losing with ignoring her and her shit, but I was trying to hold onto not falling into her trap today.

"Yo big headed ass can sit there and act like you can't see me and keep ignoring me if you want to. I'm getting tired of your shit Brodrick!" I was standing my ground and was still looking through my phone. She was not about to rattle me today and she was not about to get a rise out of me. I was tired of arguing about shit that she already knew the answer to. She let out a hard sigh as she came over to the bed area and snatched her phone off the nightstand and her charger out the built-in socket on the nightstand. I wanted to laugh out loud so bad but that would only fuel her fire. Honestly, I wanted her to leave so I could finally move. It was really hard to stay ignoring her when I knew she was mad for no reason. She was upset that I hadn't heard her request and just like that all my hard work had been tossed out the window. When she finally stormed out the room with her bag thrown over her wrist, she took the three-second walk to the front door and slammed that mu'fucka hard ass shit. I finally exhaled the breath I had been holding in before I shook my head and started getting ready for the remainder of my day. It was safe to say I wouldn't be seeing Mia until she got out of her feelings.

Chapter Fifteen

-Mia-

Brodrick had me fucked up! I peeled off into traffic, and my tires screeched as I pulled out of our condominiums parking lot. Going straight to the nearest Chick-Fil-A, I grabbed me some chicken mini's, a lemonade, and a chicken biscuit sandwich. I was eating for two now and I already had the appetite like I was eating for more than me before I got pregnant. Yeah, I had just smashed the food he had made for us but now the baby was hungry. I was hell bent on keeping this baby. I didn't care how much money Bandy threw at me; I was not getting another abortion. After two prior procedures to terminate my pregnancies, he had me fucked up if he thought I would let him talk me into doing shit else that would result in me being hurt and mad. I was no longer living for Brodrick O'Neal, he had eaten his cake these past four and a half years and he had robbed me two times of being a mother.

While some girls wanted to be astronauts and models growing up, I wanted to be a mother and a wife. I had been bred to be a homemaker; my mother was a stay at home wife the entire time my brother and I was growing up. It wasn't until my brother J.R. and I went into high school that our mother, Contessa, went and got a job as a secretary at a spa. She had grown within the company and had shown us and our dad what a strong black woman could really do besides make bomb ass family dinners and construct Halloween costumes. She was the woman I strived to be one day. It had been her love and motivation that pushed me to go to college and obtain my degree in Social Work.

I was nearing my last and final semester at USF and I was glad to be headed in the right direction. The experience I had with the girl Destiny in the bathroom yesterday, showed me what I was getting myself into with this career choice. I knew she was pregnant the minute I saw her damn near run to the bathroom. I had listened to her empty her stomach and I almost joined her, but I fought back my urge to throw up. I couldn't imagine what she could be going through. Here I was at thirty with my own dilemma involving an unsuspecting pregnancy, except Bandy and I hadn't been making sure he wouldn't shoot my club up. We had been two adults willingly playing Russian roulette every time we laid down with one another. I wasn't mad with myself though, I was disappointed and mad at Brodrick's response to yet another "fuck up" as he would describe it. I was so happy that my womb could still produce a baby. For some strange reason, Bandy wouldn't budge on our discussions in regard to us starting a family.

He had hinted at marriage before he ever brought up us starting our own family. I was actually ecstatic that after all the trauma my body had endured, the Lord still saw it fit to plant a life in my womb. I couldn't stop thinking of all the possibilities a baby brought to my life.

While Bandy was racked up and had invested his money in the right avenues, I didn't need him for his financial stability. My parent's, my father more so, had set our futures up well before either J.R. or I could talk let alone walk. Our parents valued a strong educational background and we only went to the best schools. It wasn't until high school that they allowed us to go to a public school where the real culture shock took over. There was so much going on at the public school that our sheltered upbringings had not prepared us for. I couldn't remember how many people asked if my hair was my hair when I first entered at Lakewood High school. The boys wanted to play in it and the girls wanted to fight me because of it. While J.R. was more hipped to the street shit, he kept a watchful eye on me and eventually I caught on how to blend in with the other students. I had been so green freshmen year and went home several days beggin' my mama to send me back to private school but my mama did her whole motivational speech thing after reminding me a few times that going to public school had been my idea, and I was going to see it through. That talk alone got me through some of my toughest days. I was sitting outside my secret apartment, smashing the food and not caring what was going on around me. I had spent the last few nights here trying to get over the last fight Bandy and I had, only to be right back here because of another one. I was getting tired of trying to motivate a man, who claimed he loved me, to start a family and be about them and me. I deserved more. I finished the food and tossed the crumbled wrapper and box back in the bag it came in.

I fumbled with holding my bag, keys, and my half-drunk lemonade. When I successfully got the key in the hole and turned the locks, I let out a sigh. As the cool air that circulated around in my apartment slapped me in the face, I kicked off my sandals and dropped the keys on my entry table. I took a long swig of my now watered-down lemonade as I finished it off. I had expected that Brodrick and I would have probably spent the day together or something but after his latest stunt, I wasn't checking for that nigga at all. I could spend my day catching up on my ratchet tv shows or finishing my final papers. My productivity level was on a solid ten and not Brodrick, nor anyone else could alter that. I decided to do both as I gathered my school stuff and made a beeline to my living room. I grabbed a bottle of my alkaline water and a bag of multi-colored carrots and some ranch before getting comfortable on the couch and booting up my laptop and going to my DVR list to catch up on my latest episodes. I decided on *Black Ink Crew: Chicago* as I logged into my laptop and gained access to my school's online portal. I had been writing my final paper on google docs and wanted to finish the paper. I had strong research points and I had even gone into the field. Hell, yesterday had been an impromptu field test because I had to be quick on my feet. I was going to step into my new life as a social worker and save a few lives in the process. I listened as the usual bullshit went on between Ryan and his employees as I dove into completing my final paper.

Four hours later and a half-eaten pizza from Dominos sat on top of my closed laptop. I was three spoon scoops into some moose track ice cream when my phone alerted Bandy was calling. I knew it was him from the stupid alert tone I picked for him. I rolled my eyes at the phone as I let the call ring to voicemail, I would have liked to just forward him but that would have been too easy. I wanted him to think I was out somewhere kickin' it. I knew where I was, and I was the only one that needed to know where I was.

Besides, my parents and my brother nobody knew about this apartment downtown. My daddy knew Bandy preferred me under him, but my dad insisted on having his own stake in controlling my life still, just like Brodrick. It was like they were both having a pissing contest to see which of them could control my life best. This was the only thing I let my dad control. He paid the bills in this luxury studio apartment and I couldn't tell Bandy shit about it or my dad would disown me. Let him tell it, this was his way of keeping me close. I didn't care what he did to stroke his ego, I was more than fine with keeping a secret place away from Bandy. He had been really working my nerves lately, and I was starting to feel like our relationship had begun to run its course.

I was scraping the last lil bit of ice cream out of the pint-sized carton, when my text banner revealed a text from an unknown number. I didn't give my number out and only a select few even had my number. I started to ignore it but seeing as Bandy was too lazy and not willing to call me from his business phone, it wasn't him. I could only pray that one call would be all I heard from him today. I pulled the notification box down and clicked on the new message and started reading and quickly responded.

727-303-5356: Hi Ms. Mia, this is Destiny. I got your number from the other receptionist at the rec center, I hope you don't mind. I wanted to say thank you for your help yesterday.

Me: Destiny, Hi! How are you?! It's ok that you got my number, I was super worried about you yesterday, a lot of people were. And no need to thank me, I did what I would want done for me if it happened to me

727-303-5356: Smiling Emoji

Even though I was getting ready to step into the world of social work, I didn't know what to respond back with. Bandy and I didn't send emoji's very often and when we did, he would overuse the eggplant and water drops. I sent back the same one and hit the button to turn the screen off. I had grown tired in a matter of hours and I wasn't going to blame the being growing inside of me for my sudden desire to hibernate. I grabbed the throw that I kept on the couch for this very reason and got myself nestled under it. I let the tv watch me as I dozed off to sleep.

Chapter Sixteen

-Destiny-

When I fainted yesterday, I just thought I was fatigued or something but hearing that I was pregnant shocked me and not to mention, Coach B heard with me. I told them he could stay in the room. As soon as they informed me of my diagnosis, I instantly regretted allowing him to hear something so private about me. He left out the room like I had disappointed him or something. I mean he was the coach, but he wasn't my daddy or nothing like that to be casting his judgement on me. I had to be released to my guardian, so I had to wait until my grandma showed up to get me. I was waiting for her for almost forty-five minutes when she finally came to get me. The ride home last night had been spent with me tuning her out as she called me every name but a child of God.

I was so happy when we made it home and seeing a sleeping Nero and Zai on the couch helped me out more because she refused to wake anybody up for this. I recoiled to my room as fast as I could and went to bed. Forgetting who my grandma was, she was with all the theatrics this morning; showing out as soon as Nero made his presence known. I had already been up eating a bowl of cereal when she came in. She just mumbled something under her breath and proceeded her daily routine of making coffee. I had time to get the lady at the rec's number and sent her a text. When Dinero's dark face came into view, she turned it on. Calling me many of the epithets she had used hours prior, also adding a few new ones. I was feeling high key embarrassed. I wasn't embarrassed that my cousin knew I was pregnant, I was embarrassed that my own grandma would be doing all of this.

Yes, I'm young and have no fucking idea what I'm going to do with a baby, but I do know I'm going to weigh out all my available options. I have an inkling of who it could be, but I am also a lil fuzzy on dates, so I really need to sit down and figure all this out. I had been sitting in silence this whole time, compartmentalizing all the shit my grandma was spewing out of her mouth. If I decided to go through with this pregnancy, I promised that I wouldn't be like her or even like my own mother. I didn't have the opportunity to see if she would have become a better mom. My early childhood and even up until she died had been rough. I was swearing right now to go hard in the paint for mine.

First, I needed to narrow this daddy list down. It was times like this that I wished I was more careful with who I laid down with. While I have had pregnancy scares in the past, none of them compared to this moment right here. I had finally been caught and now weighed down with so many scenarios and possible outcomes. While I knew a baby would hinder a lot for a sixteen-year-old, I was mentally equipped with my own life experience to assist with raising a child. I was drawn briefly from my own thoughts as the boys ran up out of here at the first opportunity to do so. They asses didn't even say bye, but I wouldn't hold it against them. My grandma did the most all the time.

Seconds later, my sister came into the kitchen my grandma was gearing up for another roasting session brought to you by my life and I was supposed to sit here for a third time and be belittled. Tah, I thought not! I rose from the chair that I was sitting in and proceeded to leave the kitchen. Before I could put one foot in front of the other, my grandmother's voice froze me.

"Sitcho ass down you lil hoe, I ain't say yo ass could leave."

My sister looked from our grandma to me back to her. I sat my ass down and prepared mentally to shut down as she proceeded to ridicule me.

Chapter Seventeen

-Dino-

The years had turned into months, then weeks and now a nigga was days away from breathing fresh free air. I had already started giving away my shit I didn't want. I had waited a long time to see this day. I owed it to my seed and Celeste. I had a whole forty-eight hours left in this hell I had been forced to live in. I had been spending my last days sorting through shit and mentally preparing for stepping back out in society. I was more than sure shit had changed on the outside. Just from the little bit of shit I caught on the little ass tv they had in this bitch; I could see the world was much different from when I first stepped foot in here. I wasn't scared though. I had remained solid even when niggas had opted to hate on me. I could live with their deceit but the time away from my boy was what had truly fucked with me.

A friend of a friend got word to me that Dinero was really knees deep in street shit and slowly was making a name for himself. I couldn't imagine what my son had seen and done and personally I didn't want to know. I had grown up as a black boy addicted to the street life, so I could only begin to imagine what he had been going through. I really had failed him, catching all this time had taken me out of his life. I really just felt like Celeste would have been there to guide him in the right path. I really never thought she wouldn't be here once I finished this bid. Shit was crazy how life worked out sometimes. I was worried that my son was too far gone and he was instinctively doing what was embedded in his blood.

I would spend the next two days saying my goodbyes to men that had been here with me my whole bid and a few that had entered while I had been here. I hated leaving these men behind, but I had done my time and was more than ready to get back to my life. While it would be different stepping out, I knew I had a few favors I could call when I touched down.

Two Days Later

I allowed these two days to come and go. When the guards came to get me, I had skipped everything but reciting my number at count this morning. I didn't want to eat another meal out this mu'fucka or even take another shower. I saw the last fifteen years flash before my eyes as the process was now reversing as I redressed in the Pelle Pelle fit I had on when I had entered years ago. I knew for damn sure this shit was outdated and I would need to jump right into the current fashion trends as soon as I got into the free world. This fit was too snug for my physique now and a nigga could barely walk out this mu'fucka. I was processed out and walked my black ass out the door, looking into the faces of correctional officers I never wanted to see again. As I walked the distance it took to get to the official exit where you were no longer encaged, I took one last look at the hell hole I had finally rose from, and continued walking until I was finally seeing a clear sky without looking through a chain link fence. An M&M Blue Audi TT pulled up.

She expeditiously hopped out the car and ran over and hugged me. When we detached from our hug, I took her in with my eyes. She was standing there at 5'4, with thickness for days. Her hair had grown since the last time I laid eyes on her; she had it in a twist out style. I hadn't expected her to be available to a nigga when I got out but here she was, coming to pick a nigga up and shit. We got into her whip and I took my last looks at the acres of hell as we rode off the property and onto the open road. It would be an almost four-hour drive before we reached St. Pete.

Mia had been the girl I couldn't let go. She was honestly the one that got away. Yes, I was with Celeste and while I loved her with all of my heart, she didn't give me everything I needed and desired as a man. Now that she was no longer here, I wished I would have cherished our relationship more. I looked over at Mia as she drove down the country ass dirt road that was leading us to the paved highway. She looked over at me with a girlish grin.

"What chu looking at?"

"I'on even know but when I find out, I'll let you know," I retorted jokingly

She playfully punched my arm as she navigated her whip.

"So old boy must be handling his business if you pushing this," I said, taking in the leather details and craftsmanship of the vehicle.

"Why I can't just be doing this for me, nigga," she said while sucking her teeth.

A chuckle escaped my body, further taunting the lil attitude she was trying to have.

"I'm just saying he gotta be doing something right. You look nice and shit. Hell, the last time we spoke you was talking marriage and shit. You really crushed a nigga heart with that one," I said, pouting for dramatic effect.

She cut her eyes at me before busting out in laughter.

"You hungry?" she asked. We were well away from the prison now and a nigga had been fasting for this very moment. While it would probably just be fast food we were grabbing, my insides had digested far worse, so I had to see what a Big Mac was hitting for fifteen years later.

"I could eat," I replied as she continued for a few more miles before veering off the highway and to the closest restaurant. As usual, it was a McDonald's right off the exit, and nothing could control the way my mouth was watering.

She grabbed the first available space and pulled in. But once she looked inside and saw how swole the mu'fucka was, she put the car in reverse and headed for the drive thru.

I shook my head at her, ain't shit had changed bout her. She was still a no nonsense kinda girl and she rarely bit her tongue.

"You want your usual?" she asked, never taking her eyes off the menu board.

"You don't know my usual but if you do, I'll take it."

She sucked her teeth again before saying our order to the person on the speaker.

"Umm yeah lemme get a number one with no lettuce and extra Mac sauce, sprite for the drink; and can I also get a twenty-piece nugget meal with a coke, and sweet and sour sauce," she said and we listened to the worker recite our order. Once she insured everything was correct, we drove around.

"Damn!" I exclaimed as we neared the window

"What wassup?" she asked with concern etched across her face

"Man, it's nothing big I wanted a chocolate shake," I said, causing her concerned look to be replaced with a smile.

"Nigga it's nothing, we can order it whenever they open this damn window," she verbalized as she put her attention on the workers inside joking as we waited for them to take our money. When they finally came over to get our money, she added on the shake and we proceeded to the second window to get our food. When the drink carrier ended up in my lap, I was geeked about the milkshake cup being see through, I was so entertained by this. Even McDonald's had changed on a nigga! I could see what was in my shit!

Mia laughed at how excited I was about this small thing. If she found this amusing, she would probably be laughing at my ass for days.

We continued with our drive as I enjoyed my favorite meal. She knew a lot about me and hadn't forgotten it. I fucked with her more for that. I hoped that we could get our bond back how it was before I got locked up, but a nigga knew it wouldn't be easy with Mia having a man and all. We drove and talked the remaining two hours catching up on everything.

Chapter Eighteen

-Dinero-

Patience was grinding her petite ass into my lap as my meat sat safely housed in a magnum. I had been denying myself the relief I needed all for the almighty dollar. I hadn't seen my bitch in days, and she was showing me how much she missed a nigga. Her siblings were out in the living room tearing shit up while their mom was working a double at the assisted living facility she worked at. My girl was the quintessential example of a hot girl. She had done a lot for a nigga since I met her, and I was going to ride with her pretty ass until the wheels fell off.

The splacking sound was so loud that it would have normally caused those on the other side of the door to knock but the way this 2 Chainz album was set up with the surround sound system that I got her a while ago, no one could hear shit. I was close to burstin' and she was well into her fourth or fifth orgasm. If my mama could see me now, I'm sure she wouldn't approve of the way a nigga was living and I'm more than sure she would have had a lot to say about Patience.

She was looking up into my eyes as I slow stroked her. With every moan that escaped, I got closer to releasing.

Once I felt her muscles tighten around my piece, I could no longer contain myself. I wasn't a pro at sex yet but the older women I had encountered--thanks to Tone and Dash-- had been getting me caught up with how to please a female. I felt myself release as I looked down at Patience who wore a satisfied look on her face. I got off of her and rested my Retro 11's on the ground as I carefully pulled the rubber off. She got up and retrieved her robe off the floor where it had been tossed upon us starting. I admired her body as I used the baby wipes she kept to clean my piece off. I had to go make a play and I definitely didn't wanna smell like rubber, nut, and pussy.

"Why you staring at me like that?" she asked with a grin.

"Damn I can't take in your beauty?" I joked.

"Well when you put it that way..." she said, seductively walking over to me. I didn't have time for another round, but Patience had her ways of making a young nigga stay.

"Man, don't bring yo freaky ass over here trying nothing, we just went at it for bout an hour," I said with a chuckle.

She instantly sucked her teeth and rolled her eyes before changing her route and heading for her dresser. Pulling out a bra and panty set, she headed for the door to head to the shower that was in the hallway. I pulled my phone out and replied to a few of my buddies. As much as I hated to jet out on her, money was calling my phone. I had already mentally prepared for her to cuss me out when she came back here and discovered I was gone. I really needed to go though. I bypassed her noisy ass siblings as I headed outside and hopped in the rental Tone had gotten me while he was gone out of town.

I bought the engine to life as Key Glock's *Racks Today* blared out the speakers. I pulled off headed back north to make a few plays then head to meet up with my pops. I was excited to finally hug that nigga. I only knew him from photographs. I hadn't been raised by him; I had stopped being raised at eight when my mom died. I had been raised by the streets and it was nothing my pops was going to be able to say to deter me from getting this money. If anybody should understand it should be him, but I'd have to assess this nigga intentions when I met up with him later.

I rapped along with Key Glock as I slid north.

Brought out them racks today,

I brought out them racks today

Cartier frames on my face like Johnny Cage
Who is this lil nigga with this icy ass chain, ayy

I vibed out to my saved playlist as I slid towards the motel Tone had gotten a room for me to catch buddies at. I pulled into a damn near deserted parking lot, but I knew once I was settled in the room my phone would be jumpin' and the door would be swangin'. As soon as I used the old ass key to open the door, my phone started ringing. I stepped in the unsavory room and slid the button to pick up.

"Yooo," I answered.

I'm at the spot pull up," I said to one of my buddies before ending the call and beginning to recover all the products I had stashed throughout the room

The coke I had bagged up was still safely in the air condition vent. The sacks of weed were still secured under the rusty ass sink. I put everything on the wobbly table that was in the room along with a dingy, stained chair and a bed that was clearly on its last leg. Those were all the items that made this room even that and there probably was supposed to be a tv or something to entertain but there wasn't. I got my buddy, Chaz, who had just called his regular order. The cracka was consistent in what he wanted, and this Christina Aguilera was his drug of choice. I saw Chaz three to four times a week maybe five if he was having company.

Tone kinda gave Chaz to me as a gift for all the hard work I had put in early. I know I got this cracka simply off the fact that Tone was done with his hundred- and fifty-dollar scores plus this white boy was bat shit crazy. He didn't scare me or no shit like that, and he would die before he got a chance to ever try me. I peeked out the window like I was paranoid or some shit. I had been here the last few days making plays and now my nerves were off. I shook the feeling off and decided to take a Backwood to the head. I wished Zai was here with a nigga. He damn sure would have a nigga back but I also knew my cousin had one foot in this street shit.

Hell, I was at practice with his ass a while back. I know he could really make it playing ball. He always had a lil skills when we were jits. I just knew that this street life was keeping a young nigga paid and dressed. I wanted more once upon a time, but that shit was dead now. I just wanted the money and all the good shit that came with it. I finished sealing the blunt I had stuffed with gorilla glue and immediately lit it up. I needed to calm my nerves as I anticipated Chaz's arrival. I took small pulls off the potent blunt as I scrolled my dry ass Facebook timeline. While I loved me some Patience, I couldn't help but add some eye candy on my shit. I knew most of these hoes would die to have my baby spot, so I didn't entertain nobody, but it didn't hurt to look.

My random strolling was interrupted when Patience's picture popped up and her ringtone I picked out especially for her, started blaring out of my phone. As I started to pick up, the knock at the door drew my attention there as I got up out of the chair and made my way to the door.

"Who is it," I said with confidence.

"Hey guy it's me, Chaz," I could hear through the door.

Unlocking the door, I stepped aside as he entered. I made sure to lock the door and returned to my spot at the table.

"Wassup man?"

I picked up the bag that I put aside for him and sat it at the edge of the table.

"Uhh nothing much man just trying to have a fuckin' awesome night," he answered, shifting his eyes to the bag, but never reaching for it.

"Everything ok, you wanted your usual right?" I asked, getting suspicious. He could see me looking at his ass weird.

"Chill man I want a lil extra today," he said, weirdly rubbing the back of his head.

I shot him a glare as I started opening one of my premade bags to take more from it. After today, I was done servin' this weirdo. I had plenty more customers that wouldn't even make me miss his money. I hadn't prepared for extra, but I had to make shit work.

"How much more we talking," I asked, picking up the bag and walking near the bathroom to retrieve my scale.

"I need an eight ball and an ounce," he replied, this time less jittery. As I made my way to the sink where my scale was, I felt a sharp pain hit my left side. The bag of coke I had, fell from my hands as I went to the ground. Chaz was standing over me with a twisted smile and a butcher knife covered in my blood. My survival mode kicked in and I thanked myself for stashing a gun in the trash can closest to me. I scooted back with as much strength as my injuries would allow. Chaz was still coming towards me with the knife and he was aimlessly swinging it around. As he came to swing near my face, I felt my back hit the trash. I kicked my size twelves at that cracka's face before reaching in the garbage and producing the twenty-two.

I let off two shots, fatally wounding him before I blacked out from my wound.

Chapter Nineteen

-Desire-

The last few weeks had been crazy to say the least. I didn't stay on punishment long because my sister took all the shine with her pregnant ass. I was glad to be back doing me. Bryson's ass had been cutting up this whole time, riding the fuck out of some boy's Snapchat story. He was re-watching the boy story and clowning him. We were sitting outside on Onisha's porch in the projects. Javeeka and I had since made up and her and Nisha had even helped me swipe some shit out of Justice and Old Navy recently. The gang was back and in full effect and I was happier than SpongeBob at work at the Krusty Krab. Onisha was inside making noodles for her little sister, and Javeeka was stuck babysitting her siblings but she hadn't

missed a beat shooting all of us a text in our group chat.

Bryson seemed to have chilled on ol boy's snap story because he was no longer snickering and snorting like a damn pig. I had been scrolling my IG account when Waka's voice serenaded my ear canals. My head popped up like a jack in the box as I took in his height, his roasted chestnut complexioned skin. His deep waves that adorned his head, his Colgate white smile, and his all around swag, had me almost drooling. Bryson cleared his throat and that brought me back to Wakeem standing in front of me. I closed my mouth that I knew was hung open.

"Yo wassup, Desire?" His voice said my name so nice.

I got up off the porch and walked over to him. His teeth glistened without help from the blaring sun shining upon us.

"Hey, Waka," I said in the most flirtatious voice I could muster.

"What you doing in the jets, yo ass got a whole house to be at," he said.

He was right but shit was too hectic at my grandma's house and I'd rather run the streets with my friends.

"You know I was on lockdown or whatever," I said.

"Oh yeah I forgot yo lil ass was a klepto," he joked.

I cut my eyes at him with a fake attitude attached.

"Man don't tell me you got an attitude with a nigga," he said, flicking my nose playfully

"Stooop," I whined, swatting at him.

"Well what you doing just chillin' with ya folk," he said, nodding his head towards Bryson, who was back face-deep in his phone.

I looked at him, trying not to have any involuntary moments where I was licking my lips.

"Yea we just chillin' why what you up to?"

"Shit, Coach finally gave our asses a day off. I was hoping you'd kick it with me for a little if you can leave ya lil crew for a bit."

When I looked back, Nisha was outside sitting in the chair I had been in and talking with Bryson. I looked back at Wakeem and didn't think twice as I walked past him and down the sidewalk. He caught up with me and as we walked further down the block then he grabbed my hand.

"Come on, I wanna show you something," he said

as he had me running down the sidewalk with him hand-in-hand.

We ran a block and a half before he slowed back down to a brisk stride. I was about to start complaining when we took a short walk through a cut and then ended up at a secluded park bench.

"Ooh you done brought me to your lil duck off spot," I said slickly.

He sucked his teeth.

"Mannn stop playing with me. I come here solo

to think. You're the first person I ever bought here."

"How you even find this spot," I said, observing how the shrubs concealed the bench we were now sitting on.

"Just kinda stumbled on it one day," he said nonchalantly as he put his arm around me.

I knew I had a dumb smile on my face, but I didn't care. He grabbed my hand for the second time and intertwined his fingers with mine. I melted on the inside. I had dreamed of this moment a thousand times. We just sat in silence, enjoying each other's company for a while before we started back talking. Wakeem told me about everything he was going through with basketball and how if he didn't go pro, how he wanted to be a dentist. I found that interesting and after he confided about his crazy home life with his drug dealing uncle and his six cousins all in the same house, I felt comfortable to reveal how crazy my life had been lately, and he listened intently.

He was such a great listener and I was more comfortable with him as time seemed to slip away. We had compared our favorite shows, debated our favorite music, I had even found out he loved macaroni and cheese and he laughed when I told him I loved crabs. He joked about thot trays as crab trays here were referred to as such. I knew I wasn't a thot, so the joke didn't faze me. I loved me some garlic crabs with shrimp, potatoes, and corn. Him or nobody could shame me on that. We talked a while longer before he walked me towards my grandma's house.

When we got closer to my house, he grabbed my hand again. As I parted my lips to speak, his lips met mine and we kissed. I had my eyes closed the whole time like I had seen in movies. Just as quick as our lips met, they parted but you couldn't tell my brain that. I looked into his milk chocolate colored eyes and took him in. Even at ten I could see beyond now with Waka. He was going to be my husband. We hugged and said goodbye before I allowed the invisible cloud that I was walking on to lead me to the front door. I looked back as his smile shined in my direction. I may have been young, but I was ready for whatever came with Wakeem but only time would tell.

Chapter Twenty

-Zai-

I had been trappin all day since Coach had given the team a break. That nigga had been on one ever since our last game. While we had won it wasn't by enough points, so coach cussed our asses out and practiced our asses damn near to death. I wanted nothing more than to just rest. I needed a couple of dollars to do something special for my mama's gravesite for Mother's Day. I had been scouring the internet for the perfect flowers and I had decided on Sunflowers. I was going to make a lil cash and then take it on in. I had made a lil money today, but it was starting to slow up as the day turned to night.

I hadn't seen Nero since we were last together after that situation with the girls' grandma. I hadn't spoken to any of them now that I was thinking about it. I sent the looking eyes emoji in our group chat and waited for they asses to start texting me back. I was about to head in for the night, but I wanted to make sure they all were straight. I paid my phone less attention as I sold out of my last sack and prepared to head in. Glancing at my phone, none of their asses had responded to my text. I turned my preferred music app on and zoned out to Young Boy NBA as I walked the two blocks that it took to get to my grandma's.

It was a calm evening as I took in the sounds outside of my music.

The hood had its moments where it didn't feel like poverty or that you were unsafe. It was a safe haven for many but just as it had been a saving grace for some, it had claimed the lives of many. The streets didn't love nobody, and it often had a brutal way of showing it. I let the real shit Young Boy was talking, speak to me as I made my way home. I felt like I was just out here with nobody. It was true I had my cousins and my grams but the two mu'fuckas that had made me weren't here and they would never be here again. The thought of both my folks being gone fucked with me heavy on the regular but a young nigga had learned to stiffen my chin and take whatever punch life was bound to throw.

I retrieved my key out of my backpack and entered the house. I couldn't see my Grandma Gladys but from the sound of the theme music from Bonanza, I knew she was sitting in her favorite floral print rocker and she was glued there until the show went off. I couldn't understand why she watched a show that didn't have current episodes. It looked to have been made back before my grandma was born, so she had to have seen every episode made. I walked in the living room where my Creole grandma sat locked in. She looked over at me briefly before saying anything.

"Pitit pitit ou se lakay ou," she said in creole

"Yes, I'm home," I replied as I kissed her on the cheek and took a seat on the couch.

"You know these old bones of mine ain't like they used to be, so I had one of ladies at the church bring us food. Gone in there and fix you something to eat." She quickly stopped talking as her eyes locked back on the tv and I made my way to the kitchen. The sight of Churches chicken made my stomach somersault in elation as my mouth salivated at the sight of just the box. I washed my hands and damn near knocked the box of chicken to the ground when I saw all the damn thighs in the box. I was mad; a nigga ain't eat no ass and my mama ain't never fed me a damn thigh, and I wasn't starting now.

I instantaneously loss my appetite and reclosed the box that housed the dirty bird. I was no longer interested in eating. I would just go out later and grab me some Gyros. I made my way to my room and laid across the bed. I wasn't sure if it was from the last few days of practice or the lack of sleep I got, but I was counting sheep as soon as my head touched the pillow.

Early The Next Morning

I woke with drool leaking from my mouth and realized that I had KO'ed. I wasn't mad that I had gotten rest, but I was definitely mad I had gone to bed on an empty stomach. I was still in my same fit with my shoes on. I wiped the drool from my eyes and blinked a few times, trying to remove the sleep from my eyes. A yawn escaped my mouth as I stretched and looked around for my phone. I hadn't heard back from any of my cousins and was sure someone had responded by now. When I patted my pocket, I felt my phone and fished it out.

Destiny had responded with the one of many melancholy-faced emojis they had. Desire's rude ass had sent the sleeping emoji, and Nero had yet to respond. That shit was odd. Cuz always responded in our group chat, so I felt like something was wrong. It was a little after six a.m. and I knew it was way too early to be showing up at his grandma's house, but something didn't feel right. As I tried to calm my thoughts, Tone's name flashed up on my phone. I picked up instantaneously, expecting to hear Nero.

"Yo Zai some shit went down with Nero. I'ma shoot you an address, come there," Tone said before hanging up.

The nigga ain't even give me a chance to ask what happened but as soon as the text from Tone came through, I hopped off the bed and my feet were headed out the door. I could care less that my breath was probably on ten or that I had been thuggin' in this same outfit from yesterday. Tone said some shit had gone on but what? I know this nigga betta not be dead or niggas was going to feel me. Given it was still early, I opted to not text the girls until I had all the details. I didn't want to get them worked up if I didn't have to. The address wasn't too far from where the trap was.

When I walked up the pathway leading to the front door, all the lights were on in the house. I knocked firm but not too intimidating since I heard I was a hard knocker. I didn't want people to draw down on me. When the door swung open, Tone's face said nothing but the way he was pacing said everything. Something serious had happened and I wasn't sure if I was ready for whatever he was about to say.

He finally stopped pacing and looked at me before clearing his throat.

"Yo jit, follow me, ya people back here," he said, leading me down a hallway with nothing but Scarface memorabilia lining the walls. We made it to the end of the hall, and he opened the door and stepped aside to allow me entry into the dimly lit room. I wasn't prepared to see my cuz like he was. He looked fine, like he was sleeping. The way Tone made it seem, he was in rough shape.

"Nero, wake up!" I said, trying to wake this nigga up.

"Jitt, he doped the fuck up. He ain't woke up since I found his ass," Tone Interjected as I stood over Dinero.

"What happened he look aight to me," I said, trying to see what could be wrong.

Tone walked over and pulled the covers back, exposing the heavily bandaged right side of Nero.

"He was making some plays at the room and got caught slippin' by a buddy. I found him and brought him here. Our on-payroll doctor took care of his wound, but he sedated as fuck."

I looked over my cousin's body as Tone pulled the cover back over him. I wasn't about to leave him here. I was going to sit here until cuz opened his eyes.

"Yo I'm staying here until he wakes up," I told Tone before sitting in the recliner that sat off to the side.

"I understand, you cool here this a lil duck off I got so nobody will bother you. I'll be back in a few hours. I'll send some Uber eats or something in a couple hours," Tone said.

He said nothing else as he exited the room.

I prepared for a long day of sitting and prayed cuz opened his eyes soon.

Chapter Twenty-One

-Destiny -

Ever since my grandma broke the news to any and everyone she could tell, I had been hiding out in my room. I had no desire to interact with the outside world at all. I had been trying to contact the last guy that I slept with but had yet to get a response. I met him on Facebook, but he hadn't been active in a while. I hated that I was in this situation but I got myself into it and I refused to feel sorry for myself. I just knew I couldn't do this alone. I was up most of the night just thinking about this growing life inside of me. The response I sent back to my cousin suggested I was still feeling away about how the information came out.

I was finally getting out today though. Ms. Mia asked if we could meet for lunch and given my grandma was out and about with one of her many dates, I thought it would be best to dip out while she was gone. I was putting a coat of lip gloss on my lips as my phone displayed a text from Ms. Mia, letting me know she was outside. I did a once over in the full-length mirror before snatching my phone and PINK fanny pack off the bed. I thought to check on Desire, but she had come in the night before in a great mood and had gone straight to her room. She had her phone back now, so she was good. I walked outside and Ms. Mia was in the driveway. She smiled and waved as I made my way to her car.

I opened the door and got in. Lil Donald's voice invaded my ear canal as he rapped about a woman doing better.

"Hi Destiny, how are you feeling today?"

"I'm having a good day so far, better than last night," I said as I buckled my seatbelt and she backed out.

"Well hopefully this taco spot we're going to doesn't upset the baby," she said with a smile.

Last night had been a rough one and besides feeling bad mentally the fact that this morning sickness felt like an all-day sickness, I had yet to figure out what I could keep down. Ms. Mia's voice snapped me from my thoughts.

"I'm sorry what was that?" I asked, focusing on what she was about to say.

Laughing out loud, she shook her head as she drove towards the restaurant.

"I was saying have you had any luck reaching the dad?"

Sighing I replied, "No luck at all it's like he disappeared."

I sighed again, growing frustrated with my efforts. It was as if Ms. Mia could sense that I was being hard on myself.

"Now gone and stop all that sighing and shit, it's messed up you can't find him right now but trust and believe boo, you are not alone in this battle. You have to know I'm not gone leave your side through this."

She gave my left hand a squeeze with her right as we pulled up to a place called Èl Taco Spot. I hadn't been particularly hungry when we were coming here but right in that very moment, I could eat. We found a spot to park and made our way inside. We were seated and a few minutes later, a waitress came and took our drink orders. I scanned over the menu as my eyes landed on their three-taco combo with a side of chips and guac. Mia was just looking at me with her usual pleasant smile settled on as she sat, waiting for our waitress to come back.

"So, you like school? You're a junior right?"

"Yes, I'm a junior, and I guess I like school," I replied with a shoulder shrug.

"Well what is it that you want to do?"

As I sat and thought about what she had just asked, I had never really thought about it. My mama was a scammer and never really had a legit job or career from what I remembered. The waitress finally came back and took our orders as I prepared to answer Ms. Mia's question.

Fidgeting with my fingers, I said,

"I ain't really ever thought about it." I was being honest as hell right now. I hadn't ever had anyone ask me either, she was the first.

"Well Destiny you still have time to decide what it is that you want to do. You should just take some time to think about things you're passionate about it and go from there. If you want, I can help you do some college apps," she said.

As another waitress walked past with a sizzling plate, Ms. Mia's face changed into a disgusted expression. She was on her feet and speed walked down the aisle. I watched as she bent the corner as she reached the back of the restaurant. I got up from my seat and headed in the same direction that she had just fled to. When I walked in, I could hear her gagging as she emptied the contents of her stomach. I was fighting the urge to join her.

"Ms. Mia are you ok?" I asked with concern laced in my words.

I could hear her spit.

"Ugh, ugh yeah I'm good Destiny," she said with a sniffle as she came out the stall she had been occupying. She went over to the sink and grabbed a handful of paper towels and ran them under the faucet. She wrung out the waters and started dabbing her face and neck.

She was taking slow deep breaths to control her breathing. She used the sink to hold her up as she continued taking deep breaths then exhaling them.

"I guess I can't keep a secret either," she finally said with a small laugh.

Catching on, I replied,

"Well at least you didn't faint." We both laughed and headed back to the table. After the whole ordeal in the bathroom, I knew I was no longer hungry and I could tell by Ms. Mia's scrunched up face that she too was good on eating. She let the waitress know she could grab our check and two boxes to go. I wasn't ready to go back home. I would do anything to stay out a little while longer. I was enjoying this time with her but from the look on her face she was probably ready to go home, and I didn't blame her. Once our bill was paid and our food was securely in their containers, we headed out of the restaurant and back into the Florida heat.

The rest of the ride back to my house was spent picking Ms. Mia's brain about her pregnancy. For the most part, she was open and honest with me and I appreciated that.

The energy Ms. Mia gave off was infectious. She gave off a natural motherly vibe but learning she too was expecting, was also great. I didn't feel alone in this pregnancy journey and she wasn't someone passing judgement on me. I felt comfortable confiding in her and I knew that she was telling the truth when she said I didn't have to go at this alone.

I got out her car more willingly as I felt more relaxed. Also seeing that my grandma had yet to return was an added bonus. I watched as she drove back down the road and bent the corner. As I headed in the house, my Facebook messenger notification pinged with a message from the profile EyeAin YaMan, that was the message I had been waiting for. I got inside and plopped on the couch. I went to the messenger app and quickly read his response. I instantly saw red as I read this lame ass nigga flat out tell me that he wasn't the daddy. I started typing fast to reply, not thinking about how I came off. I knew for damn sure who I had been with and this nigga wasn't about to play me out like this. I hit send and watched as this fuck boy read my message but never responded. Fabion was his real name; I had to hang out with him a few times just to get that. He had just fucked up though and I was now about to do an extensive search via Facebook to ruin this nigga's life. Him already denying my baby was a sign that this wasn't going to be an easy journey, but I was my mama's child and one thing Stasi knew how to do was make a nigga mad. Fabion was about to feel me.

Chapter Twenty-Two

-Dino -

I had been a free man for a whole half a day, and everything was going well. Mia had allowed me to stay with her while I was getting on my feet. I was on the couch, but it was better than the beds that I had become accustomed to. I had been reaching out to my son but to no avail; he still hadn't gotten back to me. We were supposed to meet up yesterday but the youngin' never hit me up. I wasn't sure if he resented me or if he truly had gotten busy. It was nearly five in the afternoon and I still hadn't heard from him. I wasn't going to pressure the lil nigga to see a nigga though. Hell, he didn't even really know me so I could understand if he wasn't pressed to see me. I just prayed that the Lord would give me an opportunity to make things right with my son. I knew I couldn't get back the time loss, but I was willing to build upon our future. Time could only tell whether Dinero and I would be able to mend our relationship. I would wait a hundred years for my son to finally fully accept me.

Mia was taking a nap. She mentioned not feeling too well, so I had been keeping myself entertained since she arrived back home. This technology shit was giving me a headache as I tried figuring out this damn iPhone that Mia had gotten for me. I couldn't work the shit for nothing, and it was about to be a wrap because I was about to throw the shit against the wall. I was so grateful for Mia's generosity, but a nigga was out, and I needed to make something to shake. I was going to try to live legit for as long as I could. I had been hustling since I was a young nigga and the old heads had taken me under their wings, so I didn't lack the know how in getting paid. I knew everything there was to know about making fast money, but prison had taught me about patience, so I was more than ready to work a job outside the streets. I sat the phone down, and decided to give my brain time to recover from trying to figure out how to properly work that shit and flicked on the tv. I channel surfed until I found ESPN and sat back and got into *Around the Horn.*

Mia came from the back, rubbing her eyes and yawning.

"Damn didn't yo ass just wake up? How you still sleepy though?" I asked with a chuckle.

"Man leave me alone," she whined as she sat down on the couch with me.

"What's wrong witcho sick ass anyways, you seemed fine yesterday."

She looked over at me with a serious face. I could already tell I probably didn't want to hear the answer that was about to leave her mouth, but I braced myself anyways. I took attention off the tv and I watched her tuck her legs underneath herself as she cleared her throat and spoke.

"Dee, I'm pregnant," she managed to get out before she looked away like she was embarrassed to tell me or something. My stomach did drop with the news she had just laid on me, but my natural nurturing spirit wouldn't allow me to express anger towards her. I scooted closer to her and used my index finger to lift her head up from her chin.

"Why yo head down? You should be happy about this. I know how much you want to be a mom," I said, looking dead in her eyes. She looked me in my eyes, looking all sad and shit. I just wanted to kiss her lips, but I'd never violate her relationship.

"He wants me to get an abortion, I've already had two," she says somberly.

My insides were boiling, what type of nigga would put a woman like Mia through not one but two whole abortions? My jaws clench at the thought of this fuck nigga not being man enough to take care of his responsibilities. The sobs escaping Mia's body broke me from my thoughts as she collapsed in my arms and cried. I rubbed her back while speaking positive words of encouragement in her ear. I just got out but seeing her break down like this had me overly ready to catch another charge. Her face was buried in my chest for a minute before I heard soft snores coming from her. I laid her down on the couch and covered her with the throw that was thrown on the back of it. It was almost seven and I had yet to hear from my seed. I stepped into the kitchen and tried to call my son again. After the fifth ring, I gave up and opted to look through the fridge for something to eat. I settled on a beef potpie and snacked on some barbecue chips until it was done. I sat down and ate the potpie while thinking to myself. I didn't know what my boy had going on, but I don't think I could go another day without hearing from him. If the streets didn't know about Dino Debo Williams, they were about to learn very soon if my son didn't hit me up soon.

Chapter Twenty-Three

-Dinero -

"You should have just let that lil nigga die, man."

"Nah, Bandy would have killed me if I let something happen to that jit. I am growing tired of watching his ass though."

I'd been out of it for a few days, and I kept replaying the conversation I thought I heard or maybe it was a dream. It vaguely sounded like Tone and Dash. Every time it played back in my head, I couldn't differentiate if it had really happened or not. I felt drugged and I felt a lot of pain on my right side. I winced in pain as my eyes fluttered open. When I fully opened my eyes, my cousin Zai was slumped in the chair asleep. I was in a room that had minimal furniture and a dim light on. I knew I wasn't in a hospital. I try sitting up but my hand shot to my side where I was feeling pain.

"Arghh," I moaned in pain, causing Zai to wake and jump to his feet. He rushed to the bed and I swear this nigga looked like he was bouta to start crying or some shit.

"Cuz man I thought yo ass was gone die on me," he said, giving me a genuine hug.

"Goonies never say die, niggga," I responded, which caused him to shake his head in agreeance as I quoted from one of our favorite movies.

"Man, yo ass had me worried forreal. I been up the whole damn night waiting for you to even cough. Yo ass farted tho," he said with a laugh.

"Man whatever, where the fuck am I cuz?" I asked, still surveying the room.

"Tone's spot, he called me over here the next morning after you were attacked. Do you remember what happened?" he inquired.

"Dat cracka Chaz stabbed me, cuz. I had to shoot his ass." I winced in pain as I finally managed to sit up.

Zaire's eyes were wider than a bitch as he opened his mouth to most likely ask the obvious question.

"You killed him," Zai asked just above a whisper.

"Yeah and why you whispering, nigga. We alone, ain't we."

"Hell, ion know, and yeah," he replied, finally sitting back down and sighing after rubbing his hands over his face.

"Cuzzy, I want out this street shit it ain't for me no more. Coach B thinks I really have a shot at basketball, and I want to see where this shit can take me. Hell, I could be in the NBA," he confessed.

I sighed too, mentally processing what I already knew. We had been doing way too much at fourteen and Zai was excelling on the court. I knew it was going to be a matter of time before he would be on this he leaving shit.

"Cuz I knew you were about over this shit. I respect your decision though. I ain't finna let no stabbing stop me from making some cheese though cuz," I answered honestly.

"Well I didn't expect you to stop cuz, but I want you to be safe. I can't lose you, I can't lose none of y'all. I'd be a real menace then," Zai said with his head down.

I knew Zai was being dead ass serious, hell I felt the same way. I wouldn't know what to do if I lost my cousins. I looked around for my phone; not seeing it, I asked Zai.

"Yo cuz where my damn phone?" I asked, still looking around the small room.

"It's in the damn drawer, let me get it for you," he offered as he retrieved my phone out the drawer.

When my phone touched my hand, I started reading all the missed texts from Patience. I knew she was probably worried about a nigga, but I couldn't help what happened to me. I opted to not text until I was able to run down on her. I saw my pops had been blowing my phone up since he got out. And while I had been anticipating his return, I also harbored feelings I couldn't help but have. Even though I was in pain, I refused to be confined to this bed. I winced in pain as I moved about. Zai watched as I fought through the pain. As I was attempting to get out of bed, Tone walked in.

"Glad to see you up jit. How you feeling?" he inquired.

"I'm ok, just in pain," I replied, standing to my feet and stretching.

"It's normal the doc said, here take one of these," he said as he tossed an orange pill bottle at me. I caught the bottle and briefly read the name fentanyl as the pain I was feeling caused me to twist the cap back and swallowed one of the pills. I felt the effects almost immediately.

"I wanna get some work and make some money boss," I said as I collected my other belongings on top of the dresser.

"Slow down cuz, you ain't one hundred," Zai interjected.

"Jit listen to your family. I understand you wanna get back to the money but you ain't A1 right now," Tone added.

I heard them both, but I wasn't dead. Yes, I was in pain, but that shit hadn't stopped shit. It just made me want to go harder.

"Yo y'all can crash here until tomorrow, then I'ma need to lock this bitch down for a lil. This just seemed like the best place to bring you once I found you," Tone said.

"You found me?" I inquired, hoping he gave me some type of insight into the night.

"Yeah man, the shit lowkey scared me, lil nigga."

"Chaz ass had me fucked up," I admitted.

"I know you lit his ass up. We had our clean-up crew get the room back right but that cracka bled like a pig. The carpet in that room will never be the same," Tone added before pulling a pre-rolled Backwood out and sparking it.

"Boss you must have sensed I needed to smoke, it's been too long," I said, feeling relaxed at just the sight of the potent herb.

Tone passed the blunt to me and I forgot for a split second that a young nigga was almost outta here a couple days ago. Tone left the blunt with Zai and I as we got stupid high and relaxed until I felt up to leaving. I knew money wasn't everything, but I needed to be on my shit from here on out and with my head on a swivel.

Chapter Twenty-Four

-Bandy-

Mia was still on the same bullshit, but I couldn't worry myself with her longing to be a mother. Hell, she could still be one but with another nigga. Fatherhood wasn't for me, and it never would be. I loved her don't get me wrong, but I wasn't bending on this issue. If she wanted to leave, she could. I was more upset that Dinero had been wounded at the motel a couple days ago. I could have shot my own brother the day he called me with his discovery of an unconscious and injured Dinero. I knew what came with the life that each of them lived but I hadn't signed up for a thief, teen mom, and a knife victim. This babysitting job that I had assigned to myself was becoming unbearable. I'd die before I ever revealed to anyone what I had done. I was sitting in my office at the rec center going over that month's records. Donations were up and with new programs being implemented monthly, I expected a new group of kids to sign up for the upcoming summer program.

The time and work I had put in was paying off in a major way and I knew that despite my past, I had good intentions for this neighborhood. I had washed my dirty money in order to have a fresh start here at the center. I had always been big on giving back but with my girl and these kids, a nigga was way stressed the fuck out. I was wrapping up going over the numbers when a text from Mia came through

Wifey: We need to talk, are you busy?

Me: If it's about this baby shit, gone and dead that shit man, I ain't finna keep talking about this.

Wifey: Really! Fuck you! Angry Emoji

Me: Man, you tripping! I'm leaving the rec in a minute meet me at the house

She didn't reply back, but I knew her ass was going to beat me to the house. While I didn't want to have yet another conversation about the obvious elephant in the room, I would indulge her one last time. I was going to let her know that this was the final talk about it. I wasn't about to keep doing this shit with her. I finished up what I was doing and locked up. I drove the twenty minutes it took to get home and pulled into my normal spot. There sat Mia's Audi parked in its regular spot. I inwardly smiled because I missed my baby, but I already knew she was about to be on some bullshit. I could feel it in my bones. When I stuck my key in the door and walked in, I damn near tripped over a PINK duffle bag. I instantly felt my blood boiling.

"Miiiia! Where yo ass at!" I yelled through the small condo as I sat my keys on the entry table. My legs instinctively walked over to the bar and my hands subconsciously poured me a shot of D'usse. I was going to be slightly buzzed for this conversation. I took a seat on the love seat and waited for a few minutes until Mia emerged from our bedroom with two more bags hoisted on her shoulders.

"Where the fuck you going?" I asked as I took a swig of the cognac in my cup.

"Bandy, I'm done. I thought after the last three times that you would be more supportive of me proceeding with this pregnancy, but it's apparent you're not willing to compromise even for me. I love you Brodrick, but I love me more. We don't need a fucking thing from you!" she spat as she gathered the bags she had and headed out the door. I wasn't one to argue, especially about shit that I was certain I had made myself clear on. Like I said if she wanted to leave, she could. I watched as she came back inside the condo and walked past me and back in the room.

She returned minutes later with another duffle and the trunk full of makeup she occasionally wore. She stopped briefly at the breakfast nook and took her key to the condo off her key ring before sitting it on the counter. She walked back out the door like she didn't even know a nigga. I finished my drink and sat a few more minutes before getting up to have another.

It was damn near eleven at night and watching Mia just leave had put my drunk ass in a sour ass mood. Who was she to just walk out on a nigga, especially a nigga like me who had the means to keep her fine ass draped in Gucci and diamonds? I had been loving her ass for the last five years when I knew my heart housed minimum love. I started thinking about how she just left and my anger started to rise. I browsed through my phone until I found the app I was looking for.

It was a tracking app I used to keep tabs on my brother mostly and Mia when she pulled shit like she had tonight. This was honestly the first time I had to use it on her and seeing her phone ping from an unknown location had me seeing red. Where was this bitch at and with who? Had she found herself a new nigga that fast or had she been playing a nigga this whole time? I grabbed my keys and stormed out my place in search of this address. It was finally time for Mia to see the real Bandy, I had been giving her my sweet side or at least I thought I was.

I peeled out the parking lot with my mind in a daze as I cruised the empty streets in route to the destination. From my house it took about thirty minutes to get to the location. Upon pulling in, I noticed it was an apartment complex. Most people would have turned around from the look of the complex. It wasn't large enough for me not to be able to pinpoint where she resided. I drove around until I spotted the blue Audi parked outside one of the buildings. It was too late to act an ass but being the boss that I was, I opted to park a few ways down so I could peep the movement. I was drunk as fuck and while my mind was telling me to go home and charge this shit to the game, my heart was telling me to do the opposite. So, I sat and waited.

The sound of a lawn mower woke me up, and the sun was at its full potential and I thanked God for my tint. I did my best to stretch in my car. Her car was still in the same spot and it didn't appear to be any activity. I was happy that I hadn't missed this bitch being dirty, I needed proof. I sat there all of five minutes before I had to piss. Not wanting to blow my cover, I used a bottle I found in my car to piss in. Once I had relieved myself, I went on my fake Facebook page and browsed Mia's profile. She hadn't posted in almost a week and I hadn't even noticed that she had dialed back her social presence. With everything going on though, that was easy for me to miss.

I glanced up every five minutes, waiting to see who would be coming out to her car. I was not moving my whip until I had eyes on her. I decided to check on the kids via their profiles and while it was typical childish shit, I took notice to Nero braggin about cheating death. While I didn't understand why people felt the need to share every little detail of their lives, I didn't expect much from a fourteen-year-old. I strolled through the other kids' feeds just as I saw one of the apartment doors open. I put my full attention on the scene in front of me.

I watched as a smiling Mia and a nigga I had never seen before exited the apartment. I swiftly hopped out my whip and charged over there like Sonic the hedgehog.

"Oooooh so this why you left a nigga huh?" I yelled, causing a whole scene.

The smile that had just been plastered on her face, instantly went to a frown. She was still headed to her car as I made my way to her side of the car. The nigga she was with started walking around the car like he was about to check a nigga.

"Pussy boy stay, yo ass over there. This don't concern you," I warned.

"Mia you good?" the nigga asked her, ignoring me.

Who did this lame ass nigga think he was?

"Yeah, I'm good Dee," she answered

Was this bitch serious right now? I could choke this bitch to sleep! I had never beat a bitch before but today was looking like the day I turned into Ike "Beat a Bitch" Turner.

"Really shawty this how you rocking on a nigga after damn near five years, yo!" I aggressively spat my words at her.

"Bandy what the fuck is you doing!" she yelled back, approaching me.

"What the fuck are you doing! Got a nigga wifing yo hoe ass and you out here with a whole other crib and nigga. Is that jit even mine?" I said, pointing to her midsection.

I could see her entire expression go from hurt to mad in a matter of seconds. I knew a nigga done struck a nerve too cause before I knew it, Mia had gotten close enough to me where she was throwing full powered punches at a nigga's face. I was doing my best to cover my face, but her ass caught me on my nose causing it to start leaking. I had never had the urge to hail off in a bitch shit than I did right now. It was like my right hand had a mind of its own because I didn't feel it rise but I knew it was up and making the motion to hit Mia. I could see her eyes widen as she anticipated the impending involuntary slap that was coming but before it could connect, my hand was stopped mid-air.

The nigga Mia had just disrespected me in front of, had my arm and was now pushing her behind him.

"Fuck nigga, I advise you take yo hands off me and mind ya fucking business. This don't concern you," I barked in the nigga's face.

He cracked a smirk at me. This nigga had to be crazy, but he was about to see crazier.

Chapter Twenty-Five

-Desire-

The last couple days, I been walking on cloud nine with fuzzy slippers on. Waka was the nicest boy I have ever hung with. Hell, he was the only one I hung with or even showed interest in. I liked stealing more than I liked looking at boys, but Waka reminded me of Myles Truitt from the show Black Lightning. He had my young nose wide open to the possibilities of what young love could consist of. I was ready to cut class for this boy and all and I didn't give a damn if my grandma whooped my ass until I was a different race. I would risk it for Wakeem. I was meeting up with him later at the rec so he could do some solo practicing before the team arrived. I was looking forward to seeing him and woke up this morning contemplating what I was switching into after this stupid ass meeting at the school. Apparently, I could be cleared to go back if I apologized to Patrice's pussy ass. I really didn't want to, but I missed my friends. Being home alone was boring and with make-up work piling up, I'd rather look at it in school. I was gone apologize but I wasn't going to mean it.

"Desire bring yo ass on girl, I wanna get this shit over with, I got a hot lunch date!" my grandma yelled from the hallway.

I was outta my room and at the door in record time, she wasn't the only one that had somewhere to be. We got in the car and drove over to the school.

"Her apology just doesn't sound genuine," Patrice's rat face ass mama voiced.

I was trying my hardest to keep my facial expressions neutral, but I couldn't help that every time I heard Patrice lie, my face contorted in disapproval. My grandma was starting to see it wasn't me. Yes I had stolen, that bitch's shit but she deserved it. She had provoked any and all of our bad interactions and I was solely defending myself every time. My grandma had been biting her tongue, but I knew that she was minutes from having word diarrhea. I sat with my arm defensively resting across my chest. I was staring Patrice's ass down. If my stare could have killed her, she would have been lying dead on the ground. Principle Griffins was damn near the color of an apple and he must have had a headache because he was vigorously rubbing the bridge of his nose.

"Ms. Waters, while I do understand why you and your daughter are upset, Desire did apologize. I can't say I heard an unauthentic apology. I say we let the girls work it out on their own," Principle Griffins tried reasoning.

"Nah see, my daughter told me how that lil girl there be bullying her," Patrice's mother announced as she pointed at me with her chipping manicure.

Everyone else besides her and her daughter had bulging eye. Before I could open my mouth to defend myself, my grandma spoke up.

"Like this man just said, she done apologized to your lil raggedy daughter and she ain't finna do it again because you don't like how it sounded. And as far as a bully, Katrina let's not forget you and yo lil friends use to bully girls all the time, so I know for damn sure my grand baby ain't bully that burly ass lil girl. I think it's the other way around," my grandma said, causing Patrice's mom's mouth to drop open.

"Ladies there's no need for the name calling. I'm going to grant Desire back active but if she steals again from any student, she will be expelled," Principle Griffin stressed, looking from my grandma to Patrice's mom then staring directly at me. I simply nodded my head as my grandma and I stood and left. I was happy as hell. I was gonna be able to enjoy my afternoon with Waka and come Monday morning, I'd be back kicking the shit with my squad.

* Later That Day*

"So, you think I'm handsome huh?" Waka teased as we sat face to face on the bleachers, holding hands with me cheesing like a pageant contestant.

"I mean duuhhh," I coyly stated.

His Colgate smile had me in a daze. I hadn't smoked in a minute but when I was with him, I was high off his presence and didn't think about smoking. He was taking a break from doing practice drills. The way he moved on the court was like an art form. He could jook so good and had there been a person defending him, he could have scored on them effortlessly. I loved his dedication to his craft, and I was ready to sign up to be a cheerleader now just so I could cheer him on every game.

"You know you pretty as fuck to me Desire," he said, looking me straight in my eyes. Before I knew it, our lips were locked and synced. I had never been kissed before and while I was worried we weren't doing it right, opening one of my eyes and seeing Waka's fully closed confirmed we were. I reclosed mine and enjoyed the moment. I swear I could hear fireworks going off, this shit felt like what I had seen in movies. If this was heaven, I didn't want to leave for nothing. Our lips finally parted, and I took in his essence. He smelled good despite the sweat that glistened off his arms and face.

"What time yo regular practice start?" I inquired as he intertwined his fingers with mine.

"In about an hour but then I want you to meet me at our spot. I'm gonna walk you halfway home though. Let me go grab my bag out my locker," he said, gently separating our fingers. I watched him walk down the bleachers and across the court to where their locker room was. I grabbed my Betsey Johnson backpack and made my way down to meet Waka on the court. By the time I had both feet planted on the court, Waka came strolling over smiling all hard.

"Why you smiling so hard," I inquired as we walked out the gym and through the main corridor of the rec center.

"I got something for you," he proudly stated as he reached into the front pocket of his backpack and pulled out a gold basketball hoop necklace with the number four on it.

"Really Wakeem! This like your favorite necklace!" I exclaimed, admiring it as he unclasped it and motioned for me to turn around so he could put it on me.

"Yes, really Desire, you my favorite girl so you got to wear my favorite chain," he confidently voiced. I was literally under a spell with him. He stepped back and took in the sight of me wearing his necklace. He admired it on my neck for a moment before he grabbed my hand once again and led me outside to walk me halfway home.

The entire way he talked about how I was his lil baby and how we were gone be together forever. A ten, I didn't know what forever meant but it sounded like something I could do, especially with Wakeem. Before I knew it, we had reached the halfway point to my house. He didn't wanna let my hand go so we just lingered in each other's touch for a minute before he gave me a quick peck on the cheek. I had to be blushing, despite being brown skinned I was smitten as hell. I walked a little up the sidewalk, turning around to see him still watching me. I smiled at him one last time before walking the rest of the way.

When I got home, my grandma wasn't home and while she had stood ten toes down for me earlier, it was always nice to come home to an empty house. Upon entry though hearing Layton Greene's *Fed Up* blasting from behind my sister's closed door, let me know I wasn't alone after all. I went and put my bag in my room and slipped off my shoes before going to my sister's door and lightly knocking. I was usually the annoying little sister but right now I needed my big sister. When she said come in, I could tell my sister needed me too. I walked in her room as she lay on her stomach with her head propped on a pillow and tears flowing freely down her face.

"Sissy what's wrong?" I asked, referring to her with the name I used to call her when I was younger.

She attempted to wipe her face but fresh tears rolled down. I joined her on the bed and pulled my feet underneath myself, sitting Indian style.

"Nothing, that you need to worry about. Just promise me you don't ever get pregnant by a nigga that ain't man enough to step up," she expressed.

We hadn't discussed dudes or relationships in a while. My sister hadn't been talking to or about anyone lately, I knew her being pregnant had stopped a lot of her hoe-ish ways. She hadn't spoke of Rio in months and she hadn't even mentioned who the dad was. I didn't want to push her to talk, so I volunteered my information to pick her brains as my sister. Once I showed her the necklace and told her what Waka said she was smiling at me and singing stupid sing songs to me.

"Desire and Waka sitting in a tree, K-I-S-S-I-N-G, first comes love then comes marriage…" she sang, causing me to playfully roll my eyes at her before giving her a loving shove.

"You ok though sis?" I attempted to get her talking. She let out a long sigh before she sat up and propped pillows up against her headboard. As I watched her get comfortable, I can't help but stare at her stomach. She wasn't showing much but just the thought of me being an auntie had me kinda looking forward to having someone else besides Destiny. She looked down at her hands then spoke.

"I reached out to the last dude I slept with and he's basically denying the baby. I don't know what to do. Grandma be trippin as it is and I just feel like I'm gone have to figure something out sooner, rather than later," she expressed. Even at ten, I could comprehend that my sister was being faced with a pretty heavy dilemma and she probably felt alone.

"Sis forget that nigga. I'll be the damn daddy," I seriously said. It caused her to laugh and shake her head as she took in what I had just said. I was dead ass though. I knew our cousins would step in too, no questions asked. As we caught up and brainstormed together, Destiny's phone started ringing. She picked it up after a few rings. Realizing I didn't have my own phone, I stood to retrieve it but the scream that left my sister's mouth froze me in place.

"You sure?" she asked the caller through her tears. I felt my heart drop to my stomach. I was praying my cousins weren't dead or no crazy shit. When Destiny got off the phone, her eyes showed immense sympathy towards me. It was like she felt bad for me or something.

"Sissy sit," she said, patting the bed."

"What happened, Des?" I asked, ignoring her request to sit.

"Desire…" she started as she got off the bed and walked around to the side of the bed I was standing at. Wakeem was just shot, he died." I heard her clear as day as I felt the air leaving my body. I couldn't breathe. The room was now spinning, and I was headed to the floor where everything suddenly went black.

Chapter Twenty-Six

-Zai-

Nero had been crashing with me and grams and shit was like old times before our moms were murked. That nigga acted like he had been in a coma or some shit. I had already made three mini pizzas for him and he was still hungry.

"Nigga I gotta head to practice soon, you gone have to fend for yourself. Grams ain't gone make you shit cuz," I reminded him.

"Nigga I already know. I was gone roll with you until later though. I need to make me some damn money," he retorted.

"Bet, let me grab my gym bag and we can head out," I replied to him as I left out my room to retrieve my gym bag out the laundry room. Even though cuz wasn't at one hundred, he was doing much better. He didn't even make noise like he was hurting but his facial expressions betrayed him every time it was bothering him. He was waiting by the door when I got back in the living room. I kissed my grandma, who was sleeping as the news flashed a breaking news story on the screen. The caption said someone had been shot in south St. Pete and that it was a developing story. I shook my head at the tv and headed out the door for practice.

Dinero was talking about meeting his pops and while I understood his reservations about it, I encouraged cuz to have that bond. I wished I had my dad for sure. I had been robbed all around the board. As we got closer to the rec, the sirens of an ambulance zooming past us drowned out our conversation briefly. Rounding the corner, there was a crowd formed and a bunch of commotion transpiring. There were news trucks from the local station parked along the road and I could see some of the other players from my team crying and shit as we approached them.

"Yo Jay what happened?" I asked the small forward on our team.

"Man, Waka dead bro," He blurted out. I was questioning if I heard him correctly. I felt my heart racing, it felt like the wind had been knocked out of me as I stumbled back and steadied myself on the wall that happened to be behind me. Nero was trying to console me as well as stop from breaking down himself. I punched the wall in front of me, not caring if I injured myself. This shit was hitting me hard. Lil dude was a beast on the court, who was I gone assist now?

A young nigga couldn't even conceal the tears that were escaping from my eyes. Through the midst of my tears I could see Coach B arrive on the scene. Seeing him break down made the rest of the team break down. By now Nero was wiping tears from his face too. Shit was crazy as fuck. My mind was running wild at how this could have happened to such a great person. Jit was young as fuck, who would end his life like this? I could see Coach B approaching us looking an emotional wreck, there was also a bit of anger coming through as well. I tried to straighten up but given the situation, I couldn't.

Coach B made it over to us and pulled us both into strong embraces and held on for a minute. I could feel his tears dropping down on me. I knew Coach loved us, he had invested a lot of time into the team and Waka was the little brother to us all. This was a major blow to the team, and we would never be the same.

"I'm sorry this happened boys," Coach B got out through his tears. Him talking caused both Nero and I to lose it. This was going to fuck with me forever, lil bro ain't deserve this. Coach gathered up the team and had all us join hands and prayed for Waka's soul.

"Dear Heavenly father, please bless Wakeem's soul. They say we shouldn't question you and while I know it's your

will. This one is hard for not only myself but my boys, place a cloak of love around Waka's family and please give his mother strength lord. In Jesus name we pray, Amen."

"Amen," We all said once Coach ended the prayer.

"Practice is cancelled until further notice. I'll send a group text when I have more details pertaining to Waka's service. Y'all try and be strong and if you need me don't any of you hesitate to call," Coach B said as he looked at each of us in our eyes. He said his goodbyes and then hopped in his whip and peeled off. Dinero had stepped off to the side and was talking on the phone. I was trying to compartmentalize what we were about to be faced with as a team and individually. I was fourteen and the thought of dying now scared the shit out of me. Waka didn't deserve to go out like that and at only eleven years old. Like my grandma said all the time, we were living in our last days. Dinero was walking over to where I was standing and broke me from my thoughts.

"Yo cuz I'ma go holla at my pops. I know you ain't alright, but I need to get this over with. This nigga may end up being a fluke and I wanna know sooner rather than later," he confessed. I told my cousin I understood and that I'd run down on him later tonight. We dapped and he headed in the opposite direction of the crime scene. I hadn't smoked in a couple weeks and with what was going on, I was spiraling. I needed to get some bud, and probably go check on the girls. I'm sure by now they knew because between social media and living in the hood, you knew faster than the news reporters and you knew more than the cops. I was gonna go home and grab some bud and go smoke. I'm sure Desire was going crazy, it was no secret that Waka was cuz lil crush and I knew she was gone be shook by the news. I had to be there for her, we had to be there for each other.

Chapter Twenty-Seven

-Mia-

Leaving Bandy hurt like hell at first. It really did but I could no longer stay with a man that was denying me the one thing I desired. I left with my things last night just hoping that he would think about it and decided I wasn't worth losing at the last second, but our relationship wasn't a cliché. So when I got in my car and realized he wasn't chasing behind me, I drove off crying like Yvette in the movie *Baby Boy* except I had to get my own self outta there. He had shown me exactly who he was and I was finally seeing him for who he was. I was not about to back pedal either. Brodrick O'Neal had tried me for the last time. When I took off last night, I was closing the chapter of that book. I no longer wanted to know what happened at the end.

I cried the entire way back to my secret apartment. I couldn't believe that I had wasted damn near five years on someone who wasn't open to the idea of a family. He only had Tone now and even so, they weren't on the best of terms. I knew enough to know that Bandy resented his little brother for being a total fuck up at times. I didn't know the details. I knew that right before we met, he had been involved in what he called a complicated situation due to his little brother and he was just trying to rebuild. I was thankful when he stopped being in the streets fulltime and set his sights on the rec center. It gave him something positive to do with his money. When he made that move, it showed me he had matured as a man and I thought then he would be ready for a family. After the initial abortion early on in our relationship, the one that happened a year after he opened the center was the one that planted the seed in my mind that he would never be the man I married.

I could care less about the shit he did for me and more about what I truly wanted. He wasn't going to get another chance to disrespect me like that. When I got in last night, I told Dino all about it and he told me to forget about it. His exact words were, "If a nigga was really a man, he wouldn't even fix his lips to say no shit like that." And Dino was right, Bandy could yell he loved me and would do anything for me but the one thing I wanted the most, he wouldn't budge on. I was over it and was going to do what I needed for me and my future child. When Dinero finally got in touch with Dino late yesterday, his story of why he had been M.I.A was crazy. I was supposed to go drop Dino off to meet with his son this afternoon, but Bandy's antics stopped that from occurring. He had some fuckin' nerve hiding outside my shit like he had. When all the theatrics were over, a neighbor of mine said they had seen his car there all night. I couldn't believe he would go to this extent after he let me leave. I thought Dino and Bandy were gonna come to blows but thankfully it didn't, and a phone call prompted Bandy to hop in his car before it could go there. I wasn't sure what the call was pertaining to, but I saw the urgency in Bandy's eyes as he turned to damn near sprint to his car. Dino was pissed at how Bandy had come at me.

I had never seen him raise his hand to me and I would be lying if I said that shit didn't scare me, just as much as it enraged me. I wasn't expecting Dino to step in, but I also knew that he wasn't going to stand by and watch. Dino's sheer love and admiration for me wouldn't be what it was if it hadn't been for our brief fling my senior year in high school. I thought I was the shit because I fucked with him. Even knowing about Celeste and the fact that she was pregnant with Dinero. I had never laid eyes on him directly. Even though I might have heard the name a few times at the rec, but with so many kids in and out on the daily it was hard to say. I imagined he looked like his daddy, but eventually I'd get to meet him. I wanted Dino to get the time to be one-on-one with him before he introduced me. While we are strictly on a platonic level, I knew that besides not having the company of a woman that Dino has always had a spot for me in his heart, as had I for him. His love for Celeste was bigger than us hence why when he left and went up the road, I made it my business to erase what I knew of us.

Bandy caught me at my rebirth of being a side bitch and making the transition to main lady with no competition was easier, more peaceful. I wish that I knew what I knew now because trust and believe, shit would be different. I was sitting in my bed browsing over some last-minute details for this mother's day luncheon a few of the parents were putting together at the rec in the next couple of weeks. While my own mother would probably be gallivanting over the world somewhere with her rich husband, I didn't mind breaking bread with the mothers that resided in the neighborhood. With all the bullshit that was presented to them by their kids, they needed a day to relax and feel appreciated. There was supposed to be a game, and everything played between Bandy's team and a rival team from Tampa. While I didn't want to imagine running into him, it would be inevitable at his event. I planned on this being the last one I did and I'd be severing ties with Bandy and all his organizations.

Dino poked his head in the doorway. "How do I look?," he asked, doing a twirl like he was modeling. I laughed at his antics before taking him in. He sported a teal Ralph Lauren button down with khakis and a pair of Tommy Bahama stripe Asunder boat shoes. He had cleaned his goatee up and had on a pair of black and gold Ralph Lauren glasses that accented his gold teeth and his gold pinky rings. Dino was looking good enough to eat as he stood, waiting on my reply.

"You look great. Definitely, looking real Daddy-ish," I joked.

"I know I'm just going to grab a damn burger with the lil nigga but I'm nervous as shit, Mia," he confessed.

I was nervous for him, too. I was hoping they hit it off and that Dinero and Dino were able to accept each other in each other's lives. I know it would take some time and while Dino knew what came with him going to meet Dinero, I admired that he was making the necessary steps to reach out to his son. He smiled at me and let me know his ride was pulling up shortly before disappearing back in the living room. I had shown Dino all the car service apps and how to work them and he was taking an Uber to meet up with Dinero. I would have some time to myself and I planned on relaxing. I needed to really unwind after today's events. My phone brought me back from my thoughts as a text notification from Destiny sounded off. Reading her words, I broke down instantly. In the midst of me crying, I managed to text her that I was on my way. No child deserved to die and the fact that Bandy had rushed off like he had, made sense now. I quickly gathered my things and headed out the door.

Twenty minutes later, I was sitting in a room that felt like a time warp because it was nostalgic to the room I had as a teenager. There were posters and artwork all over the walls; there were bright girly colors all through the room, but the mood was melancholy. Destiny's sister, Desire appeared to be a zombie. Simply staring off in space with a tear stained face. She kept fidgeting with a necklace on her neck. Destiny had been trying to get her to talk for the longest, but no words were being spoken. I could tell she was going through it. She might have been a child, but she was hurting bad. Every few seconds, you would see the floodgates open and it was so heartbreaking. I was trying to be strong for them both and I was finding it hard to do so. Destiny was trying her best to comfort her sister. It was truly a sad scene to watch. All of a sudden, Desire hopped up with tears running down her face and she left the room. A minute later, the front door could be heard slamming. Destiny shook her head in defeat.

"I just feel so bad for her, Ms. Mia. I don't know how she feels but I can imagine. She literally was just telling me how he gave her that necklace," she said, shaking he head again.

"I have no word for what she is feeling, it has to be hard. She's young and sadly, people die. Some are young, some are old. We must rally around her and give her our love and support without conditions," I said, trying to give clarity to Destiny but her mood changed with my words. Prompting me to ask if I had said something wrong. When Destiny finally found the words, I was floored to hear the circumstances in which her sister and her came to be with their grandmother. I had no idea that they were the kids of the women killed all those years ago. I believe they started calling it The Christmas in the Trap Murders. And now that she was saying it, I was more than sure Dino's baby mama were amongst those found. My brain had that a-ha! Moment, realizing what Destiny had just revealed. My heart went out to them, the murders were still unsolved and no one even after all these years, had come forward.

This newfound information made me want to look out for not only Destiny but her sister as well. I knew that Dinero would be fine. His Dad was a stand-up guy and would make sure to fill a void I know he'd had for quite a while.

Those kids were going through so much at such a young age, I had to do my part in their lives to bring positivity and I planned on doing so.

Chapter Twenty-Eight

-Bandy-

When the call came in that Waka was gone, I nearly lost it. I was in the middle of checking Mia and that bitch ass nigga she was with but when Tone called and said what he said, I had to leave that petty ass shit alone and get the hell to my team. I knew the shit was public on social media and with how fast news traveled, I wouldn't be surprised if RIP posts were already circulating. I hit my steering wheel as I maneuvered through the city just thinking about Wakeem. Waka was the youngest on the team and had been playing basketball as long as I could remember. I remembered when his damn mama was pregnant with him. I shook my head, attempting to stop the tears that threatened to fall. Tone had texted me saying we needed to talk, and I hated talking in the hood near the trap. I never wanted one of my boys to see me there and try and find out why. They would learn really what Coach B was on, and I didn't want or need them knowing that their beloved coach was actually a big-time dealer who was also a cold-blooded killer.

I pulled up to my brother's duck off spot off Melrose and killed the engine. I checked myself in the mirror, not wanting to appear visibly going through it, but seeing my team break down killed me. I didn't want to see any of them hurt or killed. I got out my car, making sure to check my surroundings. Just because I wasn't directly in the streets anymore, didn't mean I was in the clear from getting knocked off for some past shit. I made it to the door and I knocked a couple times before the door swung open and Tone stood there high out of his mind. I brushed past him annoyed, wondering what he knew.

"Bro wassup, what you know about Waka's murder?" I came right out and asked.

Tone's eyes shifted from me, to off to the side before he started talking.

"Look bro, Waka ain't deserve that shit but Dash beefin' with a nigga from cross town and Waka was just in the wrong spot at the wrong time," my brother tried explaining before my hands wrapped around his neck. He was trying to get my grip to loosen but I had no reservations on sending the nigga to meet his maker. Brother or not.

"You niggas did this shit!" my voice boomed. My baby brother was staring into my crazed eyes as I tried to calm myself. I saw him looking helpless, but I was tired of this nigga fuckin up. Every time I let up on the reigns, this nigga and his stupid ass friend found a way to mess up. I finally let go of Tone. He rubbed his neck as he caught his breath. I started pacing the room as I was trying to figure out what to say. I guess Tone found his voice because he said,

"Bro, I'ma take care of jit funeral. I ain't know that shit was gonna go left." My brother tried to explain but I wasn't listening to what he was saying.

"You don't seem to know how a lot of shit gone go still. Not only are you going to take care of the funeral, but you gone off the nigga Dash was after and his dumb ass, too. I'm done tying up loose ends due to y'all fuck ups," I reiterated through clenched teeth. I was not in the business of repeating myself. I stared him down when he appeared to protest my request to end his best friend's life. I was not about to debate shit with a mu'fucka who couldn't handle they beef shit away from my safe haven I had created. I could no longer stand to look at my brother. I shot him one last menacing scowl before exiting out of the house and getting back in my car. It had been a minute since I smoked a phat ass blunt and given all the shit I was dealing with, I was about to come off a long ass break. I hopped back out the car and just walked back in the house to my brother sitting down on the couch when I walked in.

"Nigga gimme some weed," I demanded. Being the older brother had its perks and regardless of me checking him, he was gonna give me the weed. He got up from his spot and went off to the back of the house. A few minutes later, he returned and tossed me a half ounce of the dankest smelling weed I had inhaled. I tucked the package in my pants and headed back to the door but before I stepped out, I reminded my only sibling of our understanding.

"Good looking out baby bro, make sure you handle that shit asap. I'd hate to have to handle it myself." I saw him wear an expression of trepidation as I left. I wanted him to fear what I was capable of but him and I both knew exactly what I was on. I hated to revisit the past, but I wouldn't hesitate to revert back. I got in my vehicle and headed to the nearest stores to grab some gars and some snacks. This was about to be an awakening.

Chapter Twenty-Nine

-Dino-

Looking at my son; he looked like me. Watching him walk in the restaurant, I knew he was mine. Mama's baby, daddy's maybe didn't apply to me. It was apparent this boy was mine. I stood up and waited until he had made it to the table. I wanted to hug him, but I didn't want to scare him. I extended my arm and balled my fist, initiating a dap. He gladly obliged, sliding on the opposite side of the table.

"It's nice to finally meet you, son," I said, taking my seed in.

His naturally dark skin resembled mine, and small wicks sat upon his head like birthday candles. He definitely walked in dripping his own sauce and it looked closely like mine with minor differences.

"Sup Pops," he said, adjusting the watch on his wrist. Peeping the time piece, it didn't take a rocket scientist to know that he was blowing money fast. I was going to try and keep my feelings about him being in the streets to the back of my mind but only until I felt the need to address it.

"Nothing much son just glad to be home," I stated truthfully.

The waitress at Chattaway's came over with our drinks and took our order. Lil dude ordered a Dr. Pepper like me and shit. We both laughed when we said it in unison. He was definitely my seed through and through. We were kicking the shit and getting reacquainted. I found out that he played basketball, he hadn't made a nigga a grandpa yet, and without me even asking he told me all about his lifestyle. While I listened to my son gloat about the money he was seeing, a part of me wanted a piece of the action and the father in me opted to try and reason with my son.

"Dinero, sometimes fast money ain't always the best money," I stated honestly.

He looked away from his phone before acknowledging me.

"Pops I hear you but what you really saying to me? You and mom were criminals and hell, I like what I'm doing. I done been off the porch for three years now," he said, looking me square in my eyes.

"Son you're currently recovering from a stab wound. You let a buddy get you," I tried painting a clearer picture for him.

"Yeah but that cracka dead now," he stated coldly as the waitress walked up with our entrees.

I was still stuck on how nonchalantly he said the guy who stabbed him was dead. I realized at that moment I wouldn't know my own son. I watched as he sat his phone down for the first time since arriving and closed his eyes briefly to say grace. I followed suit, bowing my head and saying my own silent prayer over my food. When I looked up, Dinero was smiling at me.

"What?" I chuckled.

"Nothing, just didn't take you for the type to pray and all," he answered.

Wow, my own son thought I was some shitty ass human or something. I thought to myself. I thought I was actually a decent person, but it be your own family that made you question. I bit into my burger and I swear my mouth watered. McDonald's had nothing on a Chattaway's burger, and I was tempted to order one to go.

"Are you still cool with Shad and Stasi's kids?" I inquired. Not sure how they are but hoping they straight."

With a mouth full of food, he started talking, which is a pet peeve of mine, especially while I was locked up. I couldn't stand for someone to talk with their mouth full and even worse while I'm eating. I was going to mention this once and hoped my son fixed it.

"Yo son, don't even talk to me until you done chewing and swallowing your food," I said bluntly.

He closes his mouth and proceeded to chew his food before speaking to me.

"Damn my bad Pops. Yeah, them my cousins for life, and I'on usually talk when I eat like that. I got manners and shit, my mama raised me semi right," he admitted. I was glad to know my boy had some respect and that me checking him didn't cause any tension. I was nervous so I knew he was too and watching our similar mannerisms was throwing me for a loop. I wanted to keep talking but I thought finishing our meals was probably the best route so I don't get annoyed if he accidently did something I was not used to. The rest of our lunch was spent talking sports, music, and our favorite bitches off whatever season of Love & Hip Hop was out. Yeah, a nigga was up on the current season thanks to Mia and while I really rather watch ESPN, I indulged in what I dubbed as ratchet tv, a couple nights with her.

"Yeah my lil baby be making me watch it with her ass all the time. I hate to admit it but as these women say, I know all the tea." my son laughed, making a reference to a new popular phrase I was still trying to understand.

"Only tea I know is Lipton son," I replied as we both shared a laugh.

Our lunch was a success and when we left out, we promised to meet up again soon. The hug me and my son shared felt real, it made me feel like we could actually have a relationship. I watched my fourteen-year-old son got into the driver seat of a car and peel off. I really wanted to fix the bond with my son, and I would first have to get him away from the niggas that had him thinking he was Nino Brown Jr. It was one thing to mentor him and it was a whole other thing to send him down a path of no return. I was home now, and I'd be damned if a bunch of nobody ass niggas who opted in the destruction of their own community, would trick my seed off the streets. Dinero was never gonna go into the system as long as I was free and had breath in my body. I had already done it for him, he didn't have to have the experience. I stood outside the restaurant, waiting for my Uber to arrive. Mia had already texted me that she would be out a while longer, so I had time to chill at the crib.

As I sat in the backseat of the Uber, I took the quietness as a time to reflect on my day. I recalled almost having my gangsta tested earlier, hell I felt tried. That fat ass nigga Mia called her man, had definitely crossed the line. When I saw that fuck nigga raise his hands to her, I didn't even think about the fact that I was fresh out because I was willing to go back in for this nigga really trying her in front of me. It was niggas like him that had real ass, down ass, women but they treated them like shit. Thank God Mia had sense because I wouldn't be cool with her staying with a nigga like him. I had heard enough in the last few days about the nigga that didn't sit right with me. When she came home last night in tears, all I could do was keep it blood raw with her. She didn't deserve the shit he was putting her through, it was simple as that. I didn't have to tell her she deserved better, shawty knew she did. I continued thinking as the driver pulled into the complex. I fished the spare key that Mia gave me days prior, out of my pants and entered the dimly lit apartment. Mia told me it was a honeycomb hideout that her dad insisted she had. He wasn't wrong in getting her a place to come because from the looks of things, she needed it. I just hoped she was fully done with him.

The love I had for Mia was abundant but sadly it did not trump my love for Celeste. They both had put up with my shit. Celeste had loved my dirty drawers since our freshman year at Osceola High and for that she would always be my rider. Even in death, she would always be a part of me, looking at our son confirmed that. Mia had been a senior at Gibbs High school when I met her. I was twenty, and in the streets heavy. I would take her to the mall and splurge on her ass but soon after I met her, Celeste ended up pregnant. I was torn between the two, but I knew I had to do right by my seed but as everyone could see that shit didn't pan out like I thought. Had I not trusted the niggas I was around, I would have never been indicted on the charges of drug possession with intent to distribute and sell. They basically tried to say a nigga was Frank Lucas and, in all actuality, I was far from that. The lil weight I was moving was nothing compared to other niggas that I was around. I had made a shit ton of money, but I didn't have a snitching bone in my body when they booked me. I caught all that time because I refused to give up names. I wasn't going to be labeled a snitch, not then, not now, not ever.

You would think the niggas I use to run with would have helped a nigga with commissary or something but the thing about being locked up is, you learn fast who with you. All them niggas turned they back on me even after I stuck to the g-code. I was solid as fuck but them niggas were not. When you were behind them walls, it's like everybody outside of them forget about you. I was brought out of my thoughts when I heard Mia entering the apartment. I could hear her drop her keys on the entryway table.

"Dee you up?" she called out to me.

"Yeah, I'm in the back," I replied back.

She walked into the den style room that had become my temporary room. She sat down on the couch next to me. Shawty was looking hella despondent, so I slid closer to her and pulled her into a strong embrace where she immediately broke down and started crying. I didn't know what was troubling her, but I wanted her to have this moment. She had been going through a lot lately and this breakdown she was having was inevitable. She cried on my chest for almost fifteen minutes before she finally wiped her tears.

"I'm sorry, I'm all over the place right now," she confessed.

"No need to apologize beautiful, it's been a rough week."

She let out a sigh as she began to explain where she had come from. Hearing that a child had lost his life probably behind dumb as street shit infuriated me, but the shit happened more often in poverty-stricken environments then those who weren't familiar with the harsh realities that black people faced every day. This news alone made me want to get a grip on my son before he too fell victim.

Chapter Thirty

-Desire-

It's been two and a half weeks since I was involuntarily forced to say goodbye to Wakeem. I hadn't said much of anything to anyone. Even my grandma had been respecting the fact that I had nothing to say. It's like my voice left when he left. Nobody could have prepared me for such a blow though I had never lost anyone at my age, losing Waka hit me hard. I hadn't had a loss this big since my parents and it hurt just as bad. I never even got to say goodbye to him. It was like one minute we were sharing our first kiss then the next, I was sitting a few rows behind his mother watching her break down in a church. I had been visiting our secret spot since he died. I came here the night he died, hoping his death was a hoax but when I arrived, I knew it wasn't. I broke down that night but had been making slow progress in letting him go, even though I'd never fully forget him. I was sitting on the bench surrounded by bushes just rubbing my finger along the necklace he gave me. I hadn't taken it off for nothing, not even to bathe. At this current moment, I was feeling overwhelmed though. Mother's Day was Sunday and I am not handling it well at all. No matter how much time passed this feeling never got better; each year gets harder. It never seemed to get easier. I knew my cousins and my sister wanted to go by their grave sites but I didn't want to. I just was not in the mood to deal with the rollercoaster of emotions that I had been dealing with. I feel like death had been around me for so long and it's still lurking. I wanted to grow up and live beyond the normal life expectancy.

I was on Waka's Facebook account, looking at old pictures and videos of him. His mom had since made the page a remembrance profile, so his old post where buried under tons of condolences and people reminiscing. Perhaps I was causing myself to stay in this slump because I visited his page anytime I was missing him, which was often. I hadn't even been with my friends, which they had all reached out on numerous occasions, but I wanted to be alone. Mentally, it was tormenting to think that while I knew plenty people either loved me or had love for me the people, I feel like loved me the most weren't here. My mama and daddy meant the world to four-year-old me. I could still vividly see my daddy playing with me at the very house I had grown to call home. Ten-year-old me felt cheated like God had hand-selected me to inflict pain on me. I was angry at my current situation, my feelings, and my life in general. Why did Waka have to die so young? Why did I have to figure life out alone? So many questions and thoughts had been formulating in my head the last couple weeks. A text to our cousins' group chat pulled me from my self-inflicted sadness.

Zai: Y'all going to the luncheon thing Saturday?

Sissy Pooh: If it's food involved, y'all know I'm coming! Plus, Ms. Mia will be there too.

Nero: Nigga you going?

I hadn't even considered going, I didn't like the idea of being reminded I didn't have a mother. The shit high key pissed me off. I was tired of being one of four token faces for kids who didn't have parents anymore. The shit really brought my mood down and being a kid alone was hard enough. People thought we wanted sympathy but really, we just wanted our peoples back. I didn't want to be charity; a project for someone to add to their list of taxable donations. I was going to hold off on replying because I really wasn't sure if I even would be participating in much of anything this year. Between my sister's impending debut into motherhood and my cousins disclosing the fact that Dinero had been stabbed by a buddy was even more indication that life was going too fast for us. A girl hadn't even been in the mood to steal let alone plot on the idea of stealing from anyone. I felt like I was going through another phase that would probably result into a new trait or habit I wouldn't understand. It was like the world forgot that I was a little girl when it started tossing B.S. my way. I deserved to be happy and right now, I was the furthest thing from happy. As the day transitioned to night, I finally managed to walk myself home. The hood was still live and while my grandma always would tell old stories of how my daddy use to have to be in by the time the streetlights came on, there were still kids younger than me playing outside. The block was still live with the local dope boys serving their buddies and hoodrats arguing loudly on their phones. I pushed all of it to the back of my mind as I made my way home.

Destiny was braiding my hair for me as she talked to Ms. Mia on her phone. I wasn't sure of what to make out of Ms. Mia at first, but she had been very supportive, more so than my grandma and for that she had won me over. I just hadn't vocalized that yet. She was attentive to our needs as individuals. She still hadn't met our cousins, but we planned on introducing them soon. I could hear their whole conversation since my sister had her on speaker.

"You girls coming Saturday?" Ms. Mia asked.

"Yeah, we'll be there," my sister announced, gripping my hair for the next braid.

I still wasn't sure but leave it to my sister to say yeah. Before I could protest., Ms. Mia was giving us the rundown of how it was going to go. The mention of possibly hitting up the mall after, piqued my interest and ultimately curved me from saying no. The rest of their conversation was about Destiny's no-good baby daddy, who was already causing my sister stress. Allegedly, he asked her to have an abortion but that struck a nerve with not only my sister but with Ms. Mia as well. My sister had disclosed that Ms. Mia was expecting too but she had no details besides she was keeping the baby, no dad's name, no boyfriend, just that she was expecting. I thought it was a good thing for my sister to have someone to go through this with. She needed the support right now. Our grandma wasn't supporting her decision to keep the baby and even if that meant more money from the state, she felt like the baby would require her to leave her lifestyle alone to be a great grandmother and to her, she was too young to be a great grandmother. I stretched my legs as I looked at the zig zag braid design my sister put in my head, It wasn't what I wanted but it would do.

"You know I'm trying to get my certificate for hair braiding," she proudly stated, looking over her work.

"Yeah well, it straight but next time do something your customer will like," I joked.

She stuck her tongue out at me accompanied by one of her middle fingers. I laughed before retreating to my room to finally get some sleep.

Chapter Thirty-One

-Mia-

"Dinnnnno!" I yelled out from the bathroom. I was bleeding profusely in the shower. I had felt the pain but ignored it. What I was experiencing now could no longer be ignored.

"You good?" Dino's voice invaded the fogged-up bathroom.

"Nooo," I stammered out, the pain was too much.

"I'm calling 911," he sounded panicked.

"I, I'm having a miscarriage. Dee don't call," I managed to get out with tears now flowing down my face. I had enough homegirls to tell me what it was like, but I never thought I'd be experiencing one myself. I was feeling defeated; even God didn't want me to have this baby. At the first sign of me being able to leave the shower, I did. Fifteen minutes later, with Dino by my side, we pulled up to St. Anthony's Hospital.

"You gone get signed in, I'll park," he said as I walked myself inside. The waiting room was empty as I walked up to the kiosk they had for patients to sign in. It was nearly three a.m. and I hoped this would be quick. As I sat, Dino was walking in looking so handsome. He wore this serious expression on his face but as he got closer, it registered more as concern. He sat next to me and grabbed my hand. He softly and slowly used his left thumb to caress my hand. I was trying to think happy thoughts, but I knew that eventually my unsavory thoughts would win. My name was called a short while later and once the nurse checked me out, she confirmed what I already knew. I silently cried as Dino rubbed my back as we waited for the nurse to return with further instructions. This pregnancy had been a highlight in my life and even if we weren't going to be together, I felt the need to let Brodrick know that I had lost the baby. After the nurse explained some of the things I may go through in the following days, I was discharged and headed back home.

Back at home, I was being catered to by Dino and I was loving every minute of it. He wasn't helping me out of obligation; he wanted to help me, and I appreciated that. The Mother's Day luncheon was later today, and I wasn't in the mood. I was mourning the loss of my baby and the last thing I wanted to do was celebrate Mother's Day. Dino was trying to tell me to skip but after finally falling asleep and waking at ten, I had made a promise to a few of the women at the center and I was determined to fulfil my obligation and finally be done with Bandy. I took a thirty-minute shower just trying to feel clean after going through the miscarriage earlier. I was mentally preparing to be amongst mothers and kids today and I was hoping I got through it. I was going to do a simple wash and go today and wear my olive green and mustard colored halter top jumpsuit that I had gotten off Zaful. I paired a pair of gold Tom Ford sandals and put a coat of clear gloss on my lips. Dino was leaning on the door frame admiring me.

"You make the simplest shit look sexy," he complimented as he licked his lips. I hadn't been looking at Dino like that but right now, he looked like a whole three course meal as he stood wearing nothing but a pair of basketball shorts and a pair of white Nike socks. His golds glistened with no assistance from the light.

"You not too bad looking yourself," I smirked, grabbing my fanny pack and strapping it onto my waist.

"Be strong queen, and when you get home, we'll just chill and watch movies or something,"

"Sounds like a plan," I said as I walked past him, heading out the door.

The rec's multipurpose room was decorated so beautifully. Me and several other rec workers had only spent all yesterday setting up, probably how I ended up losing the baby. I pushed my negative thoughts to the back of my head as I greeted and smiled, shaking and hugging familiar faces that I had grown to like and love. The turnout was great, and I had successfully not run into Brodrick. It was like he wasn't there, but I knew his ass was. I knew the boys were playing in the tournament, so I knew he'd be making his appearance sooner rather than later. I wanted to give him the news in private, so I excused myself from a table full of matriarchs and headed towards Bandy's office. As I got closer, I could hear an argument going on inside the office. Even with the music coming from the multipurpose room, the conversation was loud enough to be heard. I wasn't one to snoop or try and gather information, but no one could have prepared me for what I heard next. Jesus himself could have come down and told me I would hear what I heard, and I would have questioned it. I could have sworn I heard movement coming from a janitor's closet a few feet away, but I shrugged it off thinking I was too hype eavesdropping.

"Have yo ass here after the fucking game Tone! I told yo simple jack ass to handle that nigga Dash! He the reason I'm down a fucking player right now! I'd hate to have to finish some more shit that you failed to complete."

The phone conversation ended as my mind was trying to piece together what I heard. I wondered if this was how detectives were when they were investigating a case. I was so caught up in trying to figure out what the last part meant, I didn't realize he had opened the door. Bandy stood, looking down at me with an equally surprised look on his face.

"Everything iight? The mothers good?" he asked, not taking his eyes off me.

"Um, yeah everything is good, I um actually came to talk to you for a second," I managed to get out.

"Well can we walk and talk, I gotta get to the gym and make sure everything ready for the game," he stated dryly as he locked up his office and walked past me.

"This is actually quick, I just wanted you to know I loss the baby earlier this morning, not that you care or nothing," I said, adding blatant jabs.

"Well thanks for informing me, I was still gonna pay for the abortion though," he coldly stated before heading down the hall. I felt my blood boiling after that last statement. I could not fathom how I had spent so many years with a man that had no remorse for my body or me. Did he ever really love me? I tried my best to fix my demeanor as I headed back to the love-filled room. I walked back in and ran right into Destiny, who appeared to be looking for someone.

"Ooohh there she go, I thought you flaked on us," she said, giving me a hug. I enjoyed the embrace for another reason. I'd break the news to her later about the baby and try to hold it together until then.

"Where's Desire?" I inquired, scanning the room for her.

"She's outside talking to Waka's mom. She's been really down lately," she admitted as she eyed the food entering the room.

"Gone and eat fatty," I said, noticing her eyeing the food

I jumped in the serving line and assisted with getting the food out. Thirty minutes later we were scraping the last out of the tin pans and cleaning up the food area as everybody finished eating. The boys were suiting up and getting ready for the game. After making sure all trash and remnants were taken care of, I went into the packed gym and found a seat next to Destiny and Desire. Our boys weren't playing at their full potential and honestly, I couldn't blame them. Ever since they lost Waka it had been rough but hearing now that Bandy knew who did it was still playing in my head. I wasn't used to the back end of the lifestyle Brodrick led prior to us getting together. He had done a great job shielding whatever he was into, from me. I wanted to ask him so bad if he knew anything, but I didn't want to make him suspicious. I may have not been raised in the streets, but I understood enough to mind my damn business.

"They losing bad," Destiny spoke, breaking me from my thoughts.

"Yeah if Waka was here, they'd be scoring," Desire expressed as she sucked her teeth.

"You may be right," I said, giving her hand a slight squeeze.

She looked up at me with so much sadness inscribed on her small face. I could not imagine losing any of my friends when I was a kid. The shit had to be unbearable for her. Talking with Destiny the last few weeks had opened her and her sister's life story up for me. This whole time I had been with the Christmas In the Trap murder's living survivors and never would have known it had I not noticed all the articles detailing the incident, pinned to the bulletin board in Destiny's room. I understood Destiny more and even little Desire. While I could tell she was still unsure of me, I could tell she was warming up to me. I had already decided in my heart that these girls would be in my life. I didn't care about them having any type of issues. I knew they lacked the love necessary and as girls, it was extremely important to instill the value of self-love. These girls had truly been through enough, and I was making the personal decision to be a mentor to them. I wasn't going to do it because I felt obligated to, I was doing it because they deserved someone in their corner.

The boys ended up losing the game and you would have sworn they didn't care but everyone knew that their spark was out. The season was coming to an end and it only seemed right that they played their hearts out but with a pivotal piece of their team gone, I over stood what these boys must have been going through. Looking courtside as the boys shook the hands of their opponents, Bandy looked visibly upset but was trying his best to conceal it. I hadn't checked on him since the day of Wakeem's funeral so despite being completely over his ass, I was going to stop by his office and check on him. I felt compelled to do so, even if he had been a total asshole to me earlier. The gym cleared out as families started leaving. I promised the girl's a trip to the mall and I was going to hold up my end of the deal. I was still emotionally and physically all over the place for obvious reasons. Tomorrow wasn't going to be easy for them or me and I'd rather spend my time making them a little happy if just for a few hours. I had the girls head home and told them I'd be by in a few to pick them up. I needed to grab the last of my things from my desk and give Bandy back the key I had. I'd also use the time to pick his brain.

Besides a few stragglers, the rec center was damn near cleared out. I made sure I had all my stuff securely tucked in my bag before heading down the same hallway that I had visited earlier that day. It was just as quiet as before, as I made my way to the same closed door. The voices inside caused me to pause as I was getting ready to knock on the door. I was familiar with Tone's voice and knew that I'd probably never get the real story if I didn't listen. I wanted to know why Waka had to die. I listened intently with my head damn near pressed to the door, paying close attention to not making any noise. I could have sworn in the midst of me being nosey once again, I saw two shadows in my peripheral but when I turned to look, there was no one there. As bad as I wanted to investigate, I couldn't leave my post as I continued to listen hoping to hear more details on Waka's murder. I got an ear full of something I couldn't believe.

"Just like I murked them bitches and that weak ass nigga for touching my shit all them years ago, I won't hesitate to put a hot one in yo ass and yo homeboy ass. I asked you to handle the shit but it's clear yo ass a weak link!" Bandy bellowed out.

"Bro you still holding that shit over my head. Yeah, we fucked up six years ago, but shit been straight. You done had a nigga babysitting they damn jits. I ain't sign up for all that. It's like you ain't trying to forget bro," Tone voiced.

My mouth had to be on the ground by now, were my ears deceiving me? They couldn't have but to make sure I listened even closer.

"You think I like killing Shad or any of them?! You and that dumb ass nigga couldn't even keep Dinero safe, and on top of that, y'all dumb ass street beef spilled too close to home. Do you know what the fuck it feels like to look in Waka's mama eyes and lie to her!" Bandy's voice boomed behind the door.

"Bro we been lying a long ass time, when you gone tell them damn kids you killed they folks?" Tone challenged.

There was silence and then I heard what sounded like a punch being thrown, followed by a lot of tussling. I took that as my chance to get the fuck outta dodge as I backed away from the door and hurriedly made my way to my car.

I needed to call Dino, I needed to tell him I knew who killed Celeste and her friends.

Chapter Thirty-Two

-Nero-

Zai and I both burst out the broom closet when the lady finally was long gone; she too got to hear the same shit we had just heard. I wanted to go in there and confront the fuck nigga off top but I also knew we needed to calculate this shit. Me and Zai took off out the rec center and neither of us stopped running until we got a safe distance away. We both were attempting to catch our breaths as Zai face displayed pure hatred. All this shit was starting to make since as my breathing settled back to normal. This whole fucking time, we had been around the mu'fuckas responsible for offing our Ogs, this shit was beyond me. I was hoping this shit was a dream but when I saw Tone duck off after the game to Coach B's office, my curiosity got the best of me. I was expecting to hear something other than what I heard but I got an ear full. I looked over at my cousin and the nigga ain't even look like himself.

"If that fuck nigga the one who killed them, I want his head!" Zai voiced through gritted teeth. As he paced back and forth. I for one, had heard the conversation between Coach B and his brother Tone and it sounded very incriminating. My mind was lowkey blown, had we really just overheard our mentor and basketball coach for the last few years confess to killing our mothers. The shit was beyond me and had me really thinking about a lot of shit now. We tried to rationalize what we really heard and it was no doubt that we were telling the girls. Given that both their parents were murdered, it was our cousinly duty to tell them we finally knew something about our parent's death. All these years without answers, standing in front of news conference cameras, all those sleepless nights we had, and their killer had been looking out for each of us. Had Coach B really murdered the one person that had always been there for me?

I couldn't sleep at all tonight, I tossed and turned as the same recurring dream kept me awake. I just remembered waking up Christmas morning six years ago after burying the charred remains of my mama and aunties and realizing that Christmas would never be the same for me. The shit had been so hard at eight years old and even now it was still hard to cope with. I often wondered if I hadn't lost my mother would I be pushing dope for one of the biggest drug dealers in the city? I would never know because my mother was never coming back. My grandma Janice was all I had in this world. My dad, who recently had gotten out from doing fifteen years and had been in jail before I was even born. He was just released a few weeks ago. Besides the occasional letters from him we didn't have any type of bond. Zai always told me I was lucky my dad was still alive because his dad had been murdered the year before our mothers when we were seven. Just like Desire and Destiny, he had no parents. To me, my dad didn't exist because he hadn't been there. Letters didn't amount to time, the nigga never let me even come see him. My mama had been all I had known besides my grandma and now with her getting older in age, I felt like I'd join my surrogate cousins in being alone completely.

Zai and I stayed in the streets and I knew my mother wouldn't approve of my lifestyle. She had always instilled in me the importance of school and being more than her and my dad, but the way life had gone it had tossed me smack dab in the middle of the vicious street life. I was going to sell so much dope I'd be able to afford everything I needed in due time. We had been out in these St. Pete streets since our eleventh birthdays, while we were far too young to be exposed to some of the shit we had been around, when the streets were raising you it was expected. I sat up in my bed staring at the newspaper article that I had taped to my wall. Looking at all five of their faces, I would never forget them. They had all been in our lives since we were born for the most part but the day that they no longer were, still hurt. If Coach B was the one responsible for ending their lives, he was going to pay for their lives with his own. On my mama, he was going to feel my pain.

I had to call my pops, he needed to know what happened to my mama, and if he didn't wanna make the move, I damn sure would.

Chapter Thirty-Three

-Bandy-

To say that I was pissed would be an understatement, it would be downplaying the obvious. Today has been shit all around the board; first, still trying to get my dumbass brother to see that his equally dumbass friend was a loose end was about to make me shoot my own damn brother. The fact that Mia dropped the bomb about her no longer being pregnant took some pressure off my mind, but it still made me wonder a few things though. She had been right at my door earlier and my mind thought for a split second that she might have heard my heated conversation with my brother, but she didn't give any indication that she had. On top of all of that my damn team losing this tournament meant I owed the opposing team's coach a band for all the shit talking I did leading up to the game. And while a stack wasn't shit, I still felt like Waka's death had heavily affected my team and that Coach Ted should have let me slide, but that was the problem with betting. The rules were set with no stipulations attached so anything could have happened, but I had made a deal so before sliding back to my office after taking the L, I slipped Coach Ted the envelope full of bills and dapped him up with minimum shit talking. I couldn't blame my boys solely for this loss, I too had dropped the ball and here I was once again cleaning up the mess.

The rec center was dark as fuck at night, given its direct location the hood could be a very scary place at night. And while most people were safely locked away in their homes, I was mentally plotting to take out my only two allies. Dash and my brother had never given me a reason to think they would fold on me but their repeated fuck ups were not sitting well with me this go around. Wakeem was eleven years old and because those two couldn't keep they shit away from where my kids were, they had to go. I was twisting the silencer on my piece as I gathered up my extra Glocks out of my desk drawer. After beating the shit out of my own flesh and blood, I let that nigga leave thinking everything was copasetic but I had determined his lack of leadership and his unwillingness to follow my lead was ultimately his downfall. Brother or not he was a liability to me, plus he allowed his emotions to put our past sins right on front streets. Thank God the building was damn near cleared out or I would have been worried if someone heard him. I had though and that was enough for me to kill the nigga right then, but I let him leave, thinking shit was sweet when it was really sour. After securing my ammo and guns, I grabbed a pre rolled Backwood from out the top of my desk and headed to my car to take this short ride to where my brother's trap sat.

Pulling up ten minutes later, I had half a joint left and I was watching the slow activity at the trap. Both Tone and Dash looked to be present since I could see their respective vehicles parked a few feet away from the house. I sat in my car a few more minutes before exiting my vehicle and making my way up to the porch. The jits sitting up there had no idea who I was and what I was capable of. I walked past them and reached for the knob before one of their dumbasses spoke to me.

"Yo ol' head what can we do for you? You can't go in there right now," he attempted to persuade me. I shot that lil nigga the evilest look as I disregarded him and proceeded inside. The old home reeked of alcohol, old food, and marijuana. I practically was navigating through a cloud of smoke as I walked through the house. I could hear voices in the back where the kitchen was. I made my way there and stopped shy of the door way. I could see Dash slumped down over the table doing a line of coke. I shook my head as I watched this dumb ass nigga get high off his own supply. I was kicking my own self in the ass for entrusting these to fucks to run my drug affairs. I stood out of sight as I listened in on their conversation now that I was closer.

"Mannnnn Fuck Bandy! I know dats yo brotha and everything my nigga, but he been stepping on our necks for far too long. Look at yo face nigga he beat the dog shit out of yo ass, ain't you tired of being Brodrick's shadow. It's time we be our own men. I met a new connect," Dash divulged before snorting another line.

"Man, you know I'm tired of being under that nigga thumb, but it ain't that easy bruh, that's family. At the end of the day, we owe the nigga, we fucked up six years ago man. This shit could have all been avoided had we had our fuckin' heads on a swivel. Plus, you got that fucking jit Waka murked. You out here living reckless as fuck my nigga. And I gotta hear bout it! The way you moving nigga is not acceptable," my brother attested.

"I'm living reckless?" I'm outchea every day in these trenches trying to live another day! I just told yo ass I found us a new connect, we can get from under yo brother fucking thumb and make some bossed up moves. Yo brother wouldn't think twice to off us nigga! I ain't intend for nobody to get hit when that shit popped off with that nigga, but that's life nigga. Just like yo brother ain't expect to have to off them bitches but he did. Them jits been a burden since he brought they asses to our attention. Got you mentoring jit, you should have let his lil ass die at the motel like I said then, that lil nigga ain't built for this shit," Dash retorted nonchalantly.

"He wanted me to kill yo ass, and I still might," my brother volunteered, now looking at Dash with disgust. While this was rather amusing, I could no longer listen in without chiming in.

"Ain't no mights baby brother, you killin' this lame ass, coked out, under achieving ass, coward ass nigga. He ain't worthy to live in this life," I said, making my presence known.

I walked into Dash and Tone's line of vision as Dash wiped the white residue from his now running nose. Shit was sickening to look at, Dash looked from me to my brother, addressing him directly.

"Man bruh, why you ain't tell me big bruh was comin' through?" he questioned Tone.

"Nigga you need to chill off that shit man, I ain't know this nigga was coming by." My brother met my gaze as he looked to be thinking what to say next.

His face was badly bruised as it housed fist marks and even an indent of my class ring. To a stranger it would have appeared that Tone had been jumped by a group of two or more but only one nigga had done that, me. I basked in my work as I took notice to the chipped tooth in my little brother's once pristine mouth. I didn't want to contain the smile that wanted to escape, so I didn't deny it as the smile crept across my face.

"Y'all probably wondering why I'm here but I want these last words I speak to be impactful. Y'all done fucked me over for the last time. Bro, I let you hang out with peon for so long yo ass slowly was looking like one to me. I heard enough just a minute ago to know that the nigga I helped raised is still in there despite who you associate yourself with," I said, cutting my eyes at Dash who was looking all crazy before I continued, "Bro, I ain't gone make you kill yo homie," I spoke evenly and calmly to my little brother, as I produced my gun with the silencer attached. I didn't hesitate or give either of them time to think before I let off two shots, one hitting Dash in his chest and the other straight between his eyes. I watched as his head hung back and I knew for sure when I looked at my brothe'rs face that his friend since sixth grade was gone. I gave him a second as he grasped what had just happened.

"I know y'all been cool for a long time but ol' boy was a liability. Hell, I thought yo ass was one too but I'm glad to hear you recognize y'all fucked up all them years ago. I can see now you was being held back by dead weight," I said, nodding my head towards Dash's lifeless body.

I made a call to our disposal crew as I fought within myself on why I hadn't ended my brother's life. I guess knowing he took responsibility for his cause that ultimately resulted in the effect of me killing them girls just further solidified that we all were fighting demons surrounding that week of terror. I just honestly thought he didn't care and had been doing dumb shit but looking at the bigger picture, it was the dead weight of Dash. As we waited for the clean-up crew, I let my brother know I didn't appreciate how jit was out on the porch talking like he ran shit.

"You gotta get these lil niggas to follow your lead, there can't be multiple leaders," I said, trying to drop knowledge on my brother.

He shook his head as if he comprehended. "I already know bro, these lil niggas hungry but they can get beside themselves. I'ma tighten up on'em next time," he replied, taking a hit off the blunt he had lit. I waited a few more minutes until the crew arrived before I headed back out to my car. I jumped in my whip and relit the blunt I planned on smoking once I had killed my brother and Dash but as I peeled off into traffic, I realized the best choice had been made. My brother was solid, and I had to trust that he wouldn't cross me. Yeah, he had brought up the elephant in the room but now I realized it was fucking with him. Just as I had a bond with Zaire, he had formed one with Dinero. It was hard sometimes realizing that we were the reasons we had these attachments to other people kids. I let my thoughts take over as I finally arrived at my condo. I walked into my crib and realized; a nigga hadn't had a home cooked meal since Mia had left a nigga. Perhaps, I should have just gave her what she wanted but I could not stomach being nobody daddy. I wasn't guaranteed to be around for her or a baby.

I neglected my hunger pains as my lack of sleep took over, and I fell asleep on the couch.

Why are you doing this Bandy?"

I couldn't believe her fine ass had really been a part of some shit like this, but I shook my thoughts away quickly. Shad was about to find out why as the tears flowed down her face like a faucet... she was visibly scared. The two corpses only a few feet away added to it. The scream was quite different when she realized Stasi was no longer with us. I had listened outside the door. I loved the shock factor when they woke up.

"Shorty, you fine as fuck but you dumb. Did you and your lil friends really think y'all were going to get away with taking as much shit as you did from my brother and his dumb ass friend?" Her mouth flew open.

"Ba... Ba... Bandy, we didn't know it was yours."

"Why would you?! Shad... or should I call you Tabitha?" Her eyes widened bigger.

"I'm... I'm... sss.. sorry," she stammered out.

"I know you is baby, you fucked up a good thing. So, tell me where's my shit at? Stasi here already told me y'all split it four ways?" I said, pointing over to Stasi's body.

"Stasi wouldn't have told you shit!" she spat.

"Really now? Her ass gave her portion to her baby daddy Devaughn, and you didn't even notice him over there in the corner," I summarized, bringing her attention over to the second body in the room.

Her eyes were damn near poppin' out her head. I could see her take a hard swallow. I pulled my gun out of my waistband and sat it on my lap.

"Bandy, please don't do this?" The tears were nonstop at this point with snot racing from her nose.

"Boo, I really hate to see you with all this snot and shit on yo face. Can you just give me what I want, so I can smoke yo pretty ass and remember you how I met you?" I said cold heartedly.

I didn't have time for her stalling; she needed to hurry up, so I could keep this party going. I had two more bodies to drop before I could watch my work on the evening news. I'd at least give their kids some closure by allowing them to bury them. I picked my gun up off my lap and pointed it square at Shad.

"Talk bitch!"

"I... I... I don't know what you want me to tell you," she sobbed.

"Oh, I think you do. But since you acting like you got amnesia, where is my fucking work bitch?" I yelled angrily as I walked over and snatched her by her weave, forcefully sliding the gun in her mouth. She tried to talk with the pistol in her mouth, and after a few seconds of being amused by her attempt, I slid the gun out of her mouth.

She coughed a bit but started speaking.

"I been spending the money, but yo shit is at my crib in my bedroom closet inside a knock off Birkin bag on the top shelf."

"Now was that so hard sweetie?" She went to speak but before she could get a word out, I fired two hot rounds in her ass and watched her fall over, her body hitting the ground with a loud thud. I left out the same way I came, in hopes of grabbing the last two in the next forty-eight hours.

I jumped up awake, with sweat dripping off me. The dream that consumed my thoughts had shook me. This was my first time every dreaming about the shit. In six years, I had never closed my eyes and saw their faces. Tonight, it was Shad and while I had genuinely liked her and had she not been involved with robbing me, she would be in Mia's position but with minor things added. I probably would have settled down back then and had some kids, but that event alone had me avoiding bitches. Mia had won me over but a couple years in, the baby talk started and had to break it to her then that I wasn't trying to be a family man. I had no regrets for what I did but I felt responsible for leaving these kids assed out. The next few hours were spent reflecting on that week and how to keep this secret. I wasn't afraid of the consequences; I was more afraid of what that would do to the kids. I rolled me a blunt before attempting to sleep again, I needed to clear my mind.

Chapter Thirty-Four

-Dino-

"Are you absolutely sure you heard that?" I asked for certainty. I didn't want to react off of hearsay. Mia had just run down her discovering who was behind my baby mama and her people being murked. I felt my anger rising at the thought of this nigga ending Celeste's life. This was the same nigga that had just been out here a few weeks ago with his nuts in his hands and his chest puffed out. I wish I had of known then and I'd probably be back in a cell living out the rest of my days.

"Dee, I'm sure, I'd never make no shit up like this. The shit made me sick to my stomach to hear him say it and honestly, his brother brought it up and his reaction confirmed it," she spoke with finality. My jaws clenched as I took in the words she spoke. By no means did I think she was lying but I was praying God gave me another sign to confirm this shit. I knew Mia well enough to know she didn't lie for shit, but this was such a heavy topic, I needed further confirmation. My phone started vibrating on the table as my son's name illuminated on the screen. I picked up without hesitation.

"Wassup son?" I asked casually, not to bring attention to my anger.

"Pops I need to talk to you ASAP? Can we meet somewhere?" Nero's voice rushed out the words.

I placed the call on mute as I asked Mia, who could tell it was urgent, if it would be ok if he came over. She quickly obliged as I gave my only seed the address and waited for his arrival. This would be their first time meeting, but it was time. While Mia and I weren't engaged in any type of thing, this would let me know if I should pursue anything with her. My son's input was necessary and wanted. The moment the text came through saying he was outside, I opened the door as he, Zaire and Stasi's girls walked up to the door. It had been years since I had seen Zai and Destiny and this was really the first time I ever saw Desire, but they all looked like their moms and the shit was so sad at that moment for me. I stepped aside as they all piled in the apartment. Once I had turned around, the shock on everyone's faces had me looking confused.

"What's wrong?" I asked no one in particular.

"Dee I know these girls and have heard of Zai because of basketball, I've seen this dark one too though," Mia spoke up.

"Yeah we do know her a lil, Zai. That's the fine ass lady from the rec," Dinero spoke, causing me to look at him crazy after referring to Mia as fine.

"We don't just know her a lil," the youngest out the clique retorted.

"Why all y'all here though, son," I said, trying to get to the meat and potatoes of their visit.

"We know who killed our parents," Destiny blurted out, causing my brain to go into hyper overdrive as I realized that this was that sign I had asked for.

"Yeah we do," Nero confirmed Destiny's revelation.

"How y'all know though?" I asked, trying to get full clarity before plotting my next move.

"Zai and I hid out in a cleaning closet near Coach B's office and heard his brother bring it up. At first we thought we were hearing shit but they also behind Waka being killed even though it wasn't intentional," Nero explained as I observed Desire looking the worse as that information was revealed.

"Well son, Mia here told me the same thing you did and now I know it to be true, I'ma handle that shit for y'all," I said, taking the lead.

"Nah Pops we wanna handle this ourselves, we the ones that's been growing up without them, excuse my language," he said towards Mia before he continued, "this fuck nigga been in our lives for some time knowing what the fuck he did. I wanna look him in his eyes when he die," my son expressed his feelings.

I couldn't let my kid go down for taking the law in his own hands. I understood where he was coming from but what kind of parent would I be to allow them to do something to jeopardize their future?

"Son, I can't let you or any of y'all do this. I'll do it," I said once again, looking at each of them.

"See Uncle Dee, I know you've never met me but you not hearing us. We want in on murking this nigga. We ain't gone never get our people back. Whatever you think you sparing us from its too late, the world already dealt us a messed-up hand," Desire expressed.

"Yeah Unc, this nigga put us all in this situation, we wanna handle it," Zaire added.

"And what you think Destiny?" I asked, to see if they all were on one accord.

"I want that nigga dead, plus It's above me now," she spoke calmly as she rubbed the pudge, alerting me that she was with child. I just couldn't believe how much they all had endured and here they were willing to avenge their moms. I thought for a few minutes before I spoke again.

"Ok I'll let you in, but this will probably put y'all mentally ahead of kids y'all age. I want us all to be smart about our next moves," I spoke as they all listened and shook their heads in agreeance. Mia went off to the kitchen to make us all food as I sat down with my new extended family and plotted on what we would do. By the time Mia had returned with fried chicken wings, fries and a pitcher of blue Kool-Aid, we had our foundation for our plan.

"Desire gone do it, she is the least expected, y'all gone hide out until she makes the signal," I instructed them.

"What the signal gone be?" Zai inquired.

"Thuglife," Nero said with seriousness etched on his face. I could tell this had been on my son's mind since getting the information. I could only imagine how they felt as they had all spent time around this clown.

"Ok Desire you gone yell out "Thug life" when you sure he's where we need him to be," I said, giving clarity.

She sat twirling a necklace on her neck as she too wore a look of seriousness. For them to be kids they wore faces of adults that had gone through a lot. It was crazy to see kids that had been forced to grow up far too soon, so consumed by street shit. But I wasn't surprised because I had grown up in the same streets, doing the same shit or worse. By the time they left out, a lot of things had been discussed and while the boys hadn't been familiar with Mia's affiliation to Bandy, it would play a major role in getting him where we needed him at. The revenge would commence in forty eight hours and while I was still hesitant to have kids handling something I could do alone, I knew this was their way of finding peace and closure.

Chapter Thirty-Five

-Zai-

The news we had gotten nearly twenty-four hours ago would have made others react instantly but we had enough smarts at fourteen to know that we needed to really think this shit over. When cuz suggested we reach out to his pops, I was sure Unc was gone tell us he had it, but Desire and Nero wanted Coach B worse than us all. Don't get me wrong, I feel played as fuck for allowing my mother's killer to condition my basketball skills but how was I supposed to know he had been around us this whole time. He had never even asked about my parents or anything now that I was thinking about it. I couldn't wait for the next two days to breeze by because we would finally have answers to questions we had only asked ourselves. I didn't know how I was going to feel looking in Coach B's eyes, but I hoped satisfaction came. I would be spending the next few days mentally preparing to add another life altering change in motion. While no kid should be thinking about killing, I wondered had Coach B thought of us before he killed our peoples? Had he been watching us out of guilt and necessity, or had the nigga finally felt bad for leaving us all motherless? So many questions and thoughts swirled around in my head.

I was looking into my mother's eyes as a moment I had all but forgotten about, flashed in my mind. I remember going to this fancy restaurant with my mama and grandma, I think it was called Ruth's Chris. My grandma had been fussing at my mama as she usually did but this time it was about the type of money my mama was spending, especially at the restaurant. I remember us leaving and I pretended to be asleep in the backseat so I could be nosey.

"Where you get money from, Shad? You just was calling me last week for a loan cause yo lights were about to be off," my grandma asked from the passenger's seat.

"Ma, you real deal trippin'. I know I called just last week to borrow money, but my luck changed last week," my mama offered.

"Shadequa... I'm your mama, I was in labor with you for sixteen long hours, and for you to sit up in this here car and lie to me is a shame. I know when ya lying girl and I know when you been up to no good. All Ima tell you is don't expect no good when you living wrong," my grandma said.

Looking back, something had been off and my grandma knew it. I put the frame down that housed her photo and went straight to my grandma who was working on a crossword puzzle.

"Zaire what you want you know I'm trying to focus on this puzzle," she said, not taking her eyes off the book.

" Nothing, just thinking about mom," I half lied, causing her to close the book all together.

"What about her?" she asked, intently staring at me.

"Just miss her," I said honestly.

"I miss her too baby, but the lord needed her more." My grandma said her usual line whenever we did talk about her.

"You think whoever did it deserve to die?" I asked her, not expecting what she said next.

"Zaire, baby I wouldn't want his mama to know my pain, it's not always about revenge. We gotta let the good Lord do His will," she said.

I could hear what she was saying but I wanted to watch Coach B die, I could see it every time I closed my eyes. I would feel better when he was no longer breathing. My grandma had since put her attention back on her puzzle book as I thought about what was about to transpire.

The fact that I had never actually killed or seen anyone be killed didn't bother me as much as it should. The anger that had since took over my body wouldn't allow me to be scared or concerned with perils that I faced. My mama had been my entire world and more wrapped in a bow. She was the one person I could rely on and was honestly the first person to see my potential in basketball even as a smaller child. I'd never taste her extra cheesy mac and cheese again or hear her hum songs by India Arie. I felt like she had died all over again, and here her killer was grooming me to be the best player. I felt like I had betrayed my mama. I know there was no way of knowing but I wanted a re-do to be able to see the treacherous snake prior to this moment. I was glad the season was over, or I would have not been responsible for my actions. Tone and his lame ass partna Dash was somehow tied into Waka's death too, shit was all bad. I just hoped my sweet mother in heaven knew that it wasn't her fault that I turned out this way, my life had been marked from birth. I would probably be repenting for the rest of my life for what I was willing to do come tomorrow. And nobody was going to stop me.

Chapter Thirty-Six

-Destiny-

This baby was finally letting me keep food down, and despite having the heavy knowledge of what was about to happen with my cousins tomorrow, I had to eat this food that my grandma had fixed, especially since she rarely cooked. She could throw down though and the smothered pork chops, garlic mash potatoes and green beans were hitting. Desire was playing in her plate of food, looking consumed with her own thoughts. I knew she was feeling all kinds of ways given Waka was involved in this. Uncle Dino had us all keeping with our same routines as to not alert Couch B or his brother. So we all were playing our best roles. The plan was to get into the rec center and wait for our moment but I wasn't sure I would be able to handle it.

I wanted to hear just like everybody else what really went down. We had never heard the story and it was necessary now. We needed that closure. I knew I wanted to know what my mama and daddy had done to be taken from us. Had Coach B known they even had kids? There were thoughts I had never even thought of but as the hours ticked away, more and more questions popped up. I had since gotten the kitchen together and was now online looking for adoption agencies. If I learned anything from binge watching 16 & Pregnant or Teen Mom, it was ok for me to give this baby up. I wasn't prepared to be a mom and in all honesty, I had only had one for ten years and even then, that shit wasn't always rosy. Adoption just seemed like the right route for me to take. It would probably bother me when I got older but what if there was a couple out there that could do more for this baby then I ever could.

I was lying in bed, rubbing my protruding stomach as I weighed all my options. I heard the front door open then close I knew it was nobody but Desire. She was probably going to where she went when she wanted to think. She still hasn't disclosed where the spot was but as long as it was helping her cope, I suppose it was ok. Our grandma was still up to her old ways, but she had been putting in the effort to provide more. She still would rather run after her boy toys but the occasional meals she had been making had been appreciated and I had been feeding me and this baby. My baby' father had all but stopped communicating with me, he had even been posting pictures with a lil redbone who had buck teeth and a lace front that made her look like Predator. She was no competition; even on my worse day I beat lil mama hands down. I had since blocked him and made the decision to give my unborn child the option of a better life. I knew that in the long run, I could potentially be giving this baby something neither of my parents could. And that was a chance.

Chapter Thirty-Seven

-Dinero-

The realest shit my pops could have done was sign off on this hit. Yeah, the shit may seem unorthodox, but our ages were simply numbers for paperwork. My mental capacity was far vaster than most fourteen-year-olds my age. I had seen and done a lot in a short period of time. A young nigga was truly a product of my environment but now knowing Coach B had created this environment for me, I was livid. I needed to know why? I had to know why. Before that nigga took his last breath, I needed to hear why he took my moms, God moms, and aunts. There was no way he'd die before I heard. I had been sticking close by the trap. I didn't wanna throw Tone off if I acted different, so I opted to go harder. I had been getting off my work as usual, and keeping my paper flowing but with an added hunger. I was coming back to re-up twice as fast as these other lil niggas and I wasn't in a race with none of them, I was securing my future. Once I no longer had to take directions from Tone, I'd be taking shit over. I had caught my first body and I felt like a man. Yeah it was to defend myself but nevertheless I had offed a mu'fucka. I no longer feared anything, I was ready to see the unknown. Patience was gone be my rider and nobody was gone change that.

I was counting the seconds when my alarm would sound tomorrow, and it would be time to suit up. Choosing Desire's badass to set Coach B in the trap was easy, once we compared our interactions with Coach B it was obvious he had neglected the girls tremendously so he would just think Desire was being genuine. Since basketball was over, Zai and I had time to grab all the supplies we needed to make this a night none of us would forget. While I probably should have wanted to forget, just like my beautiful mother, I'd never forget the day we took her killers. It was going to be etched in my memory forever. I looked up at the newspaper article as a single tear rolled down my face. I quickly wiped it away, and opened my nightstand and retrieved a pre-rolled blunt. I went to my music app and hit shuffle, the app landed on Nipsey Hussle's song *"Dreamin"* and just like that my mind shifted to the only female other than my mother who could put a smile on my face. I let the words spoken by Nipsey lift my spirits.

Patience was staring in my eyes as we shared a milkshake at Steak and Shake hours after she had been on my mind. It was late as hell and I couldn't sleep, the hours were winding down and I could hardly wait to run down on Coach B's pussy ass. When I hit her line to come out, she didn't hesitate to sneak out for a few. She was my rider and my peace, often times she wasn't even aware that she was doing a job. She kept a young nigga motivated and focused. Right now, she was giving me unconditional love. I've felt pure hatred running through my blood since I found out Coach B was behind the murders, so I needed to feel love right now. I grabbed her hands in mine and rubbed her soft skin gently. She smiled, exposing her perfectly set dimples and her flawless smile. She had on the custom rose gold nameplate with her name in cursive that I'd gotten her last year for her birthday and she had since added a matching rose gold colored "D" necklace that rested slightly below her nameplate. Her full lips were coated in a light pink tinted gloss, and the strapless romper that she had gotten in a royal purple color was making her honeycomb complexion glow. Baby girl was looking amazing.

"You know you beautiful as hell," I said, taking in her beauty.

"You know you handsome as hell," she retorted, taking another sip of the strawberry cheesecake shake between us.

"Hey don't use my line on me, getcha own!" I jokingly replied.

"I didn't! That's our line," she said as she chuckled.

"Oh that's "our" line," I said, rolling my eyes playfully at her causing those dimples and smile to reemerge.

I had been debating since sometime last week if I was going to give Patience the promise ring that I had gotten her. I knew she was the one for me, yes at fourteen I knew I didn't want anybody else. I knew that this girl was the ying to my yang and regardless of the outcome later tonight, I was going to love her forever. After my brain tried to psych me out twice, I finally lead with my heart, which housed my intentions and reached in my jeans pocket for the ring. I had my hand under the table, but I was nervous as hell as I spoke.

"Patience, you mean the world to me, girl. I know we young and all, but I don't want nobody but you, baby. It's you bae, it's always gone be you. I got you something so you know a nigga gone always be yours," I gushed as I brought my hand from under the table, exposing the ten karat gold Enchanted Disney Aladdin Pear Shaped Swiss Blue Topaz that I'd gotten from Zales the previous week.

Her eyes light up at the beauty of the ring as she hopped up and came to my side of the table before tonguing me down. I think my mans just woke up just from that kiss.

"Thank you!" she exclaimed right after she took back possession of her own tongue.

I placed the ring on her middle finger and kissed her again. I loved making her smile and meaning every word of what I said, makes it that much more pertinent for us to succeed with our plan. I paid for our shake and escorted Patience back to the car Tone had conveniently rented for me. I'd use it today and use it tomorrow to drive him to his own funeral.

Chapter Thirty-Eight

-Desire-

"Desire why are you crying? Come here baby girl. I walked over to my father, he had on an all-white linen pant suit. He looked exactly how I remembered him. He was tall, dark, and lovely as I remember my grandma describing him to her friends' single daughters. I walked over to a cloud shaped like a bench as I sat down without the cloud disappearing. I knew I was dreaming but never had I ever dreamed this vividly and especially not one that included my daddy.

"Who bothering my baby girl?" he asked lovingly.

"Nobody Daddy, I miss you. Where mama?" I asked, looking around a deserted scene.

"Welllll, I heard she in purgatory," he said before looking around the same deserted scene, as if someone else was around to hear.

"Daddy, seriously," I said, not sure what purgatory was or why she would be there.

"I am being serious baby girl, but enough about us, what's wrong?" he asked once again.

As I prepared to answer, I realize I was no longer seated next to him and that he had begun to fade away. "Daddy, wait! Come Back!"

The sun glaring down over me caused me to shield my eyes from possibly being blinded. I sat up and realized I'd fallen asleep on the bench at me and Waka's secret spot. I stretched and retrieved my phone that had fallen on the only grass spot in front of me. I had a couple text from Destiny. I texted her back first, letting her know I was fine and was clearing my mind. In a few hours, our plan would be in full effect so I stretched one more time before walking home. My dream was on a loop in my head as I tried to interpret what it meant. What was my daddy trying to say to me and what was this place purgatory? I never even knew there was such place, I just knew of heaven and hell. I got in the house with so many unanswered questions and no one to answer them. I made a mental note to look it up later as I retreated to my room to grab some clothes to shower, even though the day would be probably spent chillin, I needed to mentally prepare for what was going to happen.

The twenty minutes it took for me to shower and moisturize gave my sister ample time to post up in my room. She was laying on her side in my bed, taking a selfie when I walked in.

"Look who finally decided to come home," she joked.

"Where grandma?" I inquired, choosing to ignore her statement.

"She been gone since last night, never came back. How you feeling about today?" She answered my question while asking her own.

"I don't know how to feel honestly. I just know that even though they dying it's not gone bring mama and daddy back. I dreamed about daddy last night, it was scary. I asked him where ma was, and he said something like purgatory or something like that," I revealed.

"Purgatory is the place some say is between heaven and hell. It's said that people go there when they haven't made it into either heaven or hell. Pretty much they paperwork being reviewed," my sister explained.

I took that moment to think about this alleged middle place. If my mama was there, it was definitely because of all the crazy ish her and my aunts had done. I spent a few more minutes thinking about it before pushing it to the back of my mind. In five and a half hours, I'd be playing my role in avenging my parents, and I was war ready.

Chapter Thirty-Nine

-Mia-

I don't know how I got Bandy to agree to meet me at the rec center in a half hour but the time illuminating in my car let me know that I had to put the pedal to the metal. The sun was close to setting as I sped from the north side grabbing some last-minute things for our night. Dee and I sat up all night brainstorming effective ways to get rid of Bandy and his brother that would leave no big trace. The kids didn't know it, but Dino planned on being the one to kill Bandy, and I agreed. I wouldn't want any of them to have to live with the decision of taking someone's life, they were too young and still developing. While I didn't know all that they had been through, I knew they had been through enough. These kids deserve love and people in their lives that truly gave a fuck about them. I don't know how but I was going to make it my life's mission to make sure they all got that. Maybe my purpose had been bigger than having my own kids. Maybe I was given all these motherly traits to spread to kids that didn't get it. Everything made sense at this very moment about why he never wanted kids, he had made these kids life hell and tried to save face by putting them under his guidance. I felt sick to my stomach at the thought that the man I used to make love to, was a cold-hearted killer.

If someone would have told me I'd be a part of a plot to set up and kill the man I thought I loved, I'd tell them they were a got damn lie. I would have died for Brodrick. He probably thought no one would ever find out his secret and now that the cat was out of the bag it was about to get very interesting. I pulled up to the deserted and dark rec center as I parked closer to the door and killed the engine. I retrieved the spare key I had for the center and checked the time on my phone before getting out. It was 7 o'clock on the dot as I checked my surroundings before unlocking the door and hitting the code in the alarm not too far from the entrance. Once I locked myself in, I went to the multipurpose room's kitchen and unlocked the back door that lead in from the outside. I hurriedly turned off the lights, reset the alarm, and relocked up the center as I made my way back outside to wait the remaining ten minutes for Bandy in my car. I texted everyone in the group chat Dinero had made. I let them know everything was in place and that Dino and the boys could sneak in now. I waited until they texted back, saying they were inside.

Twelve minutes later, Bandy pulled up in the spot directly next to mine. I subconsciously rolled my eyes as he hopped out his car and walked right over to my driver side window as I dangled the keys off my manicured fingers. He wore a smug smirk as he snatched the keys off my finger.

"I see yo fine ass know how to hold a grudge but it's cool, you showed a nigga what it was a few weeks ago."

I smacked my teeth and opted to ignore his raggedy ass. I rolled my eyes this time voluntarily, as he smirked at me again before stepping back and walking around towards the center. The corners of my mouth turned up as I sent a group text and pulled out the parking lot. I couldn't wait to see his face void of that stupid as smirk. I bent the corner and Destiny and Desire popped out of a big hedge. They both hopped in as I circled back around to the center. By now it was illuminated once more. Desire prepared to get out as I stopped my car right off the city property line, it was showtime.

Chapter Forty

-Bandy-

I hadn't expected Mia to just up and leave a nigga over some baby shit but here I was taking her spare key and placing it in my top drawer. She had an attitude per usual and it was starting to not look good on her. I was more than happy to fill her position tomorrow. There were plenty of bitches that needed jobs in this city that would jump at the position and the pay I was offering. Besides grabbing my key back, I needed to go over a few things for the new season. Before I could type the password into my computer the doorbell I had installed throughout the center chimed. I looked at the time and it was nearly eight o'clock. I got up from my seat and made my way to the front of the center where Desire was standing at the door. I let her in without hesitation as she looked like something was wrong.

"Everything ok Desire?" I genuinely asked.

She put on the cutest face as she spoke, almost made a nigga smile from the heart.

"Coach B, I have a question?" she asked sweetly.

"Wassup?" I asked, taking a seat in one of the many chairs in the lobby.

She sat down too, looking me dead in my eyes.

"Did you kill my parents?" she straight up asked as she looked to be searching my soul for the truth. I on the other hand couldn't breathe, I had heard her correctly but why would she ask me that? The sound of additional voices brought me back to reality as I realized we were no longer alone. I swallowed the lump that had instantaneously formed in my throat. There in front of me stood Zaire, Dinero, and Destiny; they all wore similar grimaces on their faces as they surrounded me.

"How is it that y'all managed to figure it out?" I smugly asked.

I didn't know what a bunch of kids thought they were going to do but seeing them wear these tough expressions, I thought the shit was cute.

Dinero flagrantly pulled his Glock and tried to hit me but missed, causing his arm to drop down lower. I heard the gun go off and I knew once I felt the pain, that I had been shot. This mu'fuckin jit had shot me in my fuckin knee cap. I reached at the open wound as I looked at my exposed tendons and bones.

"You gone sitcho ass down now and answer our fuckin' questions Coach B!" an out of breath Dinero spoke.

I was in so much pain that I had no choice but to comply with their demands. If they wanted to hear the real, I wasn't going to spare one fuckin' detail. Zaire was looking at me with murderous eyes as he leaned against the wall. I went back to six years prior and told a story I thought only three people would know.

"Six years ago, I committed the Christmas in the Trap Murders. Ya peoples robbed me and I had no choice but to right their wrongs. I ain't to be robbed, they should have picked another job, but they chose wrong," I callously spoke, not giving a damn if I was offending them. They were big shit now, holding me up in the same building that I had provided a safe haven for all of them.

I was paying close attention to each of their faces as I went into full detail about how I killed each of them.

"For a nigga not in the position to be talking reckless, you sure know how to further disrespect us. You think cause you been looking out you were helping, nigga you made me and my cousins, savages. We ain't ask to be left like this. And you sitting up here like you can't lose somebody too. ThugLife," Dinero spoke loudly as I saw three figures out the corner of my peripheral.

Mia, the nigga who was with Mia the last time, and my brother walked over to us. My brother was beaten up badly, there were fresh wounds on him on top of the damage I had done days prior. The dude I didn't like dropped my brother to the ground and kicked him sharply in the side as he groaned in pain.

"Nigga, stop watching me and finish the story!" the nigga I still had no name for, demanded.

I smirked and before I knew it, Dinero had successfully clocked me in my mouth with the butt of his gun. I felt my flesh peel open as blood gushed from the wound. I wanted to scream out in pain, but I wasn't gone show nobody in this room fear. I got myself together as I talked through the pain. "Shortly after I built this place, I looked into y'all home life and decided I could help however I could. The plan was to get y'all into positive things but Dinero went a different path, and so did you Destiny. I couldn't help that the sins of your parents inadvertently turned y'all into them," I said, addressing them all. Explaining my role and my brother's role in their lives after the murder wasn't hard. I had done for them at first off sheer obligation because I felt bad, but I had eventually picked up a soft spot for all of them. I looked at Mia as she wore a face of pure disgust as I confessed my indiscretions. Oh how the tables had turned, and I had never imagined her face being on the other side.

"This whole fucking time you been mentoring us and telling us to do the right things and you're the reason we like this!" Zaire belted out as his hands clenched into fists. He ran over to me and starting raining punches down on my face. For a jit the lil nigga had some power but had a nigga been on an even playing field, I would have rocked his lil ass to sleep. Dinero and the nameless nigga pulled Zaire off of me and moved him across the room. I started laughing after a while, it was clear we weren't going anywhere. Without a warning, Dinero shot Tone in the head as his moans and groans stopped. He wore an expression of satisfaction as he turned his attention back to me. Mia stood speechless as she took in the scene in front of her. I had never known her to be into street shit so to witness her enthralled in this scene made me feel like I hadn't really known her at all.

I didn't have time to mourn my brother, I knew my time was coming or at least I thought it was.

"Son! Chill for a sec," the nameless nigga commanded.

Son? As I stared between the two faces, I now could see the resemblance between the two.

"Pop's I got it!" Nero replied, trying to reason with his dad.

"If you had it, you wouldn't have just impulsively killed him," he rebuttal back, as he pointed down to my brother's lifeless body.

While I didn't like the nigga, he was telling his son no word or lie. Plus, Dinero had been following behind my brother closely. His thought process was to shoot first and ask questions later, that was the same mindset that had helped him survive his knife attack. I wouldn't be surprised if the jit had plans of taking over my brother's trap. Hell, I know I would if I was him.

I was so caught up in the father-son moment that I had totally forgotten that Desire, Destiny, and Zaire remained with their eyes trained on me. I wanted whatever they had planned to commence. I no longer had anything else to say, it honestly was what it was. If someone would have asked me if I would have done it again, I would have done it without a second thought. Nobody was going to take from me and live to brag about it.

"Why Waka?" Desire asked randomly with sadness in her eyes.

See that I would answer because unlike their mothers, I hadn't played a role in his death. I would never put the kids in danger. Waka had been one of my favorite players and his death had hit me hard too.

"Honestly, Desire I had nothing to do with that," I honestly answered, hanging my head low.

"But you knew about it," Zaire spoke up from across the room.

I let the smallest breath escape me before I spoke.

"Y'all really think I'd hurt Wakeem, he was like a son to me." I was fighting back the tears but I refused to drop one. I was not one to cry but Waka brought it out of me. By now Dinero and his dad had tuned into the side conversation we were having.

"You know Coach B, I use to think my life was my fault but knowing what I know now, I understand how fucked up the world can be. People can be placed in your life to cause chaos and confusion and had the devil still been playing with us, we would have never known you were a wolf in sheep's clothing. You took the only thing that mattered to me at eight. I ain't ever gone get her back!" Zaire spoke through tears. Destiny went over to comfort him as he broke down on her shoulders.

"They say lil black boys are born with two strikes against them, one being the fact that they a boy and for two the fact that they black. You single handedly showed me that even someone that is seen in a good light can really be from the darkest depths of hells. You changed the course of our lives and now, you must be handled appropriately," Dinero spoke as he approached me with his father as they begin to wrap rope around me and the chair I had since been forced to sit in. By now the pain in my knee was numb, I sat as Dinero's father ensured the ropes were tight before pretty much gagging me with a sock. Mia walked over to me and whispered in my ear.

"The Hate U Give Little Infants Fucks Everybody." Before striking a match and tossing it on my lap. The fire beginning to burn my flesh finally caused me to react as I sat stuck burning alive and screaming at the top of my lungs. I watched them douse the building with gasoline and set two more fires before they exited. I watched until the smoke overtook me and everything was black.

Chapter Forty-One

The Epilogue

-Destiny-

"Desire Michelle Henry," The principal at St. Pete High announced.

"Woooo!"

"Yeahh Go Desire!"

"Go Desi!"

Our section erupted in celebratory clapping and yelling as my sister strutted across the stage to accept her diploma. She was smiling big as she shook the hands of the principal and vice principal. It had been a long road, but we were all here to witness my little sisters biggest accomplishment. Zaire and Dinero stood to the right of me with equally happy expressions etched on their faces. Patience stood to the right of Nero, holding their five-month-old daughter Dynasty as she slept peacefully through the noise. To the right of me stood my son's mom and a surrogate aunt to us all with the exception of Dinero given that her and Dino were now married. I had my baby nearly seven years ago and I decided that adoption was the best thing and after learning of Mia's miscarriage, I thought she'd make the perfect mother to the unborn child. Mia had really shown us all the love we had been missing and after we all became aware of what Coach B had done, it was crazy that she hadn't known. We all tried to recall any given moment that he had seemed off but none of us had ever found an instance. The past was behind us and as I watched the son I had gifted, cheer on his cousin-auntie as he called Desire, I now knew what unconditional love felt like and looked like. We continued cheering on Desire until the ceremony was over.

Once we made it back outside of Tropicana Field where the graduation was held, you could see families everywhere with their respective graduate taking pictures and exchanging gifts. I stood holding the balloons and brand-new Birkin bag that Desire had been begging for before this week. I stood waiting until she emerged through the crowd of people. She was glowing and smiling hard as she approached us all giving each of us a hug.

"Y'all love me huh?" she bragged, accepting all the gifts we were showering her with.

"Yeah just a lil bit lil aggy," Nero said, pulling ten crisp blue faced bills out of his pocket and handing it to her.

"Ayyyye ok cuz! Someone take my picture!" she exclaimed, being extra animated as she dropped down and squatted fanning the money out in one hand and using the other to put her pinky in her mouth to do the famous Kodak Black pose. Zai dropped down next to her after her first shot as we all took turns taking pictures with her. Once Desire was satisfied with her pictures, we all got in our respective vehicles to head to BJ's Brew House and Restaurant for dinner. Desire loved the pot stickers at this particular place so it made sense to bring her there.

Twenty minutes later, we were all being seated as our drink and food orders were taken. I took a moment to take in my surrogate family as I looked at each of them. Zaire was one of the top prospects at USF to enter the draft next year, and despite a torn meniscus his junior year, he had healed and came back stronger and better than ever. Dinero had kept his promise and had taken Patience down to the courthouse when they both turned eighteen and had made an honest woman out of her. They have been a happily married couple for the last three years and had finally welcomed Dynasty into the world almost five and a half months ago. At twenty-one the boys had grown into men practically overnight. Thanks to the guidance of Uncle Dino, who had clearly made it known he was coming to uplift us into better things with the help of Mia, had done just that. Nero hadn't been back to the block since before his eighteenth birthday and with him and Uncle Dino's barbeque business was making waves and he wasn't interested in the fast life anymore. Desire was headed to Howard University in the fall and I couldn't be a prouder big sister. She had finally crawled her way out of the slum she had been in surrounding everything that happen all those years ago. She still wore Waka's necklace faithfully and refused to part with it. I couldn't blame her and only hoped she would find someone that made her feel like he had. Rico, the precious little seven-year-old that intently stared down at his tablet as we waited for our food, had all of my features but had the purest heart thanks to Mia. He had received the nurturing I lacked. Looking at him I knew he'd be alright. Sometimes family wasn't people you shared blood with but people you experienced life with on the daily. We had made our own family despite having ours ripped apart at such young ages. Here we were all one big happy family, living life. And with our guardian angels looking over us.

The End

A Note From The Author

I hope everyone that reads this story enjoys it as much as I did writing it. It was definitely an uphill battle as I suffered from a depressive state for half of it. I made it out of that rough patch to produce something that I am not only proud of but helps give insight to issues that are otherwise overlooked in our communities or looked at as normal. I hope that readers can open their minds and hearts to the struggles that black and minority youth face everyday. It is not normal to be gunned down as a child, it is not normal to hide trauma. I hope you guys continue to enjoy my work and get ready for what's to come in the future.

-M$C

CPSIA information can be obtained
at www.ICGtesting.com
Printed in the USA
LVHW051710260220
648289LV00005B/955